Wealth of Secrets

Secrets

Stacy Angell Curtis

JoyPrint Press
ISBN: 978-1-7361231-1-9

To Walt, Ian and Cameron, love you.

When I am afraid, I put my trust in you. In God, whose word I praise—in God I trust and am not afraid. What can mere mortals do to me?
Psalm 56:3

CHAPTER ONE

Brynnan Marsh set down her menu and called her mom's cell phone for the third time. Her parents were now thirty minutes late. They were supposed to drop off a box of artifacts at a fellow archaeology professor's house, then meet her for dinner. She had no doubt they were still at Professor Drummond's home exchanging tales of their exotic travels and latest discoveries.

Brynnan, having followed in her parents' footsteps, to an extent, in becoming a historical researcher, understood the passion. But she was hungry. And had been waiting in a booth at Maudie's Tex-Mex in Austin for half an hour.

She was going to need a second bowl of chips. And more salsa.

The difference between her career and her parents' was that she did her research from the states with occasional trips abroad, while her parents lived abroad, all over the world, the majority of the time, only returning to their home in Austin occasionally. They would teach for a semester, then take off for another archaeological site.

They were in Austin for the summer, and by coincidence, she had the summer off, transitioning from a job in California to a new job in Texas.

So, she was staying with them.

For the whole summer.

It was a bit surreal since she hadn't lived under the same roof with them very often, even growing up. Their work kept them traveling. As a child, she occasionally traveled with them, but often she stayed back in Austin with a nanny.

She now held multiple degrees in history, like her parents, but she wanted a different kind of life for herself. She loved history and seeing the world, but she wanted roots somewhere. Something that felt like a home. Not that she'd accomplished that.

She kept her phone pressed to her ear, pushed her long, brown hair off her shoulders and shoved another tortilla chip into the last of her salsa.

Her mom's cell went to voicemail. Again. Had she left it in the car when they went into Professor Drummond's?

Professor Drummond's expertise was pre-twentieth century Texas. That's why they were deferring to him. Her uncle had mailed a box of artifacts to her parents for authentication, and several of the items appeared to originate from nineteenth century Texas. While her father was an expert in at least a dozen areas, nineteenth century Texas was not on of them. He was very pleased Professor Drummond agreed to confer.

Another five minutes passed.

Maybe she should just order dinner to-go and meet them at home.

Her dad's cell was usually set on silent, but she decided to try it anyway. Relief washed over her when the call was finally answered.

But it wasn't her father's voice on the phone. The voice identified himself as a State Trooper. Her chest tightened. Trying to focus on his words, panic blurred her thoughts, fogged her brain. All she remembered him saying was 'car accident,' 'ambulance,' 'hospital.'

Jack McKerrick walked through the hospital lobby, keeping in step with billionaire Marsten Kade's brisk pace. He'd been Mr. Kade's head of security for all of three whole days, and before this evening, he didn't even know his employer had any family in Austin. He researched the wealthy Kade family prior to accepting his position, and the few Kades he knew of, also billionaires, lived in Houston, the Dallas area, or internationally. He hadn't known about a brother in Austin, until tonight.

His first trip on his boss's private helicopter might have been enjoyable if the circumstances were different. But the silent tension coiled around Marsten Kade since his niece's panicked phone call kept the mood somber, and conversation to a minimum. He wasn't privy to the details from the niece's call, but apparently her parents were both in very serious condition.

Mr. Kade didn't fidget. Or wring his hands. Or even look at his phone. Instead, worry kept his powerful, athletic form unnaturally rigid, from his perfectly combed brown hair, to his perfectly polished black shoes. He was appropriately dressed to host a dinner for some potential investors at his home that evening. A dinner that was abruptly cancelled when the call came.

Jack didn't like having to insist on coming along on such a personal trip, but Mr. Kade had received several threats lately, and until Jack had a chance to ensure they were empty threats, he needed to stick close. Mr. Kade's resident IT specialist was tracking down the source of the threatening emails. Jack was hoping for an update soon.

Following signs, and maneuvering through the sterile hallways, they finally found their way to a waiting room outside of the ICU. There was only one person in the room. She stood when she saw Marsten.

His niece's appearance was not at all what Jack had expected. Sure, she was probably having one of the worst days of her life, but he still expected a young woman related to a handful of billionaires to exude, at least of hint of, red-carpet-worthy glamour. She seemed fit and definitely attractive, but her appearance was natural, not overdone.

Most of her light brown hair spilled halfway down her back, but several long strands stuck to her teary face. Her deep brown eyes, swollen with emotion were, incredibly, still striking. Grief and strength fought for dominance in her expression. He wasn't sure which was winning.

"Brynnan, sweetheart, are you okay?" Marsten asked, rushing to her side and wrapping an arm around her. "Have you heard anything more? Have you spoken with the doctors?"

She shook her head, started to speak, but hesitated. Finally, she whispered, "They're gone.

They're both gone. A few minutes ago."

Jack saw Marsten's body tense. He held his niece firmly but, didn't speak for a very long minute. Then he gently whispered to her in comforting tones while her eyes focused, unfocused, and focused again.

Brynnan allowed her head to fall against her uncle's chest, trying to draw strength from him. She'd never walked down *this* tragic road before, and yet, it felt familiar. Hurting. Numb. Confused. Scared. The unthinkable happening. And feeling so alone.

At least her uncle was there. He showed up, just like in the past. She could see he was hurting too, but she had no words for him.

Please God, help us. She didn't know what else to pray. Her mind was a fog. Was this shock? *Just please God, help me somehow.*

She wiped tears from her face, struggling to compose herself. A tall man with broad shoulders and thick, wavy brown hair stood a few feet from her uncle. He stared at her with genuine concern on his face, but she wished he'd mind his own business. If he was here to see someone at the hospital, he should keep on walking.

Marsten must have noticed her attention.

"Oh, forgive me sweetheart, I should introduce you. This is my new head of security, Jack McKerrick."

Head of security? She had no idea Marsten had hired security. He looked the part though. He was fit. *Very* fit. Maybe six two. And a little intimidating.

She managed a quiet "Hello," but she still wished he'd leave.

"I'm very sorry for your loss."

The sudden softness in his kind, brown eyes surprised her, but she didn't want to get into a conversation. "Thank you."

Jack sensed the awkwardness and decided he should give Marsten and his grieving niece some privacy. Quietly excusing himself, he retreated to the hallway—he could monitor the entrance to the waiting room from there. That was good enough. There wasn't another way in or out.

He found a vending machine nearby, purchased a bottle of water, and parked himself in a spot with a vantage point of the waiting room entrance. Marsten and Brynnan deserved all the time they needed.

His phone buzzed. It was Annalee, Marsten's long-time personal chef. Now he realized why she'd requested his number before they left Marsten's ranch. She wanted updates without bothering Marsten. Jack delivered the sad news.

His phone buzzed again. Annalee again. She made it clear she expected Jack to let her know if the staff could do anything for Marsten, and to let her know as soon as arrangements were made for the funeral. She seemed to want to keep texting but, didn't know what else to say. He understood. She wanted to do something, but at the moment, there was nothing anyone could do. He decided to take the opportunity to find out some more details about the Kade family.

He realized on the way to the hospital that Brynnan's last name was Marsh, not Kade. He was sure Annalee could explain, and she did. Jonathan Marsh, Brynnan's father, was Marsten Kade's half-brother. Different fathers.

Okay, so Brynnan wasn't actually a Kade, though she seemed close to her uncle.

Annalee's genuine grief for her boss's loss poured from her texts. Jack had noticed, before their abrupt departure from Marsten's ranch, that all the staff appeared very distraught about their employer and his family. He was still getting to know his boss so, while he hated the circumstance, the staff's sincere concern was an encouraging sentiment.

He wrestled with the offer from Marsten Kade to come onboard as his head of security for two weeks before he accepted. Though he hadn't been sure how long he wanted to stay in the military, leaving to babysit a billionaire hadn't sounded appealing to him. At. All.

But Marsten had been insistent.

They had some mutual friends. A couple of guys Jack had served with now owned successful businesses in Houston and had, at some point, befriended Marsten. Jack wasn't sure which stories were shared, or how embellished they were, but apparently during some late-night-tall-tale-swapping after a fancy fundraiser or something, his former teammates apparently shared more than they ever should have and had Marsten convinced Jack was some kind of Jason Bourne.

Marsten had recently fired his former head of security, and his entire team, in a dramatic falling-out, and wanted "only the best" for his next hire. When Marsten approached him with the offer, Jack laughed, and tried to convince him that he wasn't the right man for the job.

Jack had no doubt he was fully equipped for

the task but, protecting a Texas billionaire from paparazzi and petty thieves didn't sound very fulfilling. He'd been going after high-value targets for the past several years in service to his country. If Marsten Kade wanted a bodyguard, Jack wasn't interested.

Then Jack learned, though he'd spent most of his life in Houston, Mr. Kade had relocated to Kade Ranch, his family's one-hundred-forty-year-old country estate in Central Texas—barely thirty minutes from Jack's parents' home near College Station. His mom would be ecstatic.

And, Marsten Kade wasn't looking for a simple bodyguard. He described recent threats he'd received and incidents that had taken place over the years. Yep, this guy needed legitimate security. But was this job really the right course for him? Now?

Deep down, he knew he couldn't serve in Special Forces forever. Most people thought he should have retired four years ago instead of returning to active service. But he wasn't ready then. He completed all the mandatory counseling sessions and returned to duty as soon as he could. He needed to. Needed to prove he was still the effective leader and capable soldier he had been before the tragic mission that threatened to end him in every imaginable way.

And he pulled it off. Outwardly. In the depths of his heart and mind, only God knew how desperately he was clinging to a thread of sanity at times. But that was just it. God had pulled him through. He survived. And even returned to active duty.

He still wrestled internally, a white-knuckle grip on his faith. Life wasn't perfect, and never would be, but God had sustained him—enough to put one foot in front of the other for the past four years.

And then Marsten Kade came around making a strong case for retiring from the military. Jack considered it wouldn't be so bad to oversee security for a billionaire on a large country estate. Near his hometown. With a generous paycheck.

He could see his family more often. His two brothers were now married. His two *younger* brothers.

On the rare occasions he was brutally honest with himself, in the wee hours of several sleepless nights, he feared he would never have a chance to share his life with someone. Finding a woman willing to accept his mental burdens and emotional scars would be a very tall order. Likely too tall.

After a lot of prayer and weighing his options, he eventually decided Marsten Kade's offer was something he shouldn't pass up.

If nothing else, he could use this job to build his resume, and his bank account, and then move on to something else, if it wasn't a good fit.

He had to start reminding himself of the reasons he accepted the new position on his very first day. Because it was a doozy.

It started with gunfire.

CHAPTER TWO

On his first morning at Kade Ranch, Jack was unpacking his things in the guest suite provided for him near the security office in the main house, when he heard the first shots.

Hoping he was hearing things, but certain he wasn't, he grabbed his sidearm and ran into the kitchen to get a view from the side of the house nearest the sound of the shots. Two more shots. Four in all so far.

He scanned the property from the large kitchen windows. Motion to his left caught his attention. Two red-faced, overweight men, clad in camo head to toe, were running wildly through a wooded area behind the greenhouse. Hunting rifles clutched tightly, arms flailing, desperately navigating the mud and brush much faster than seemed possible for men of their mass—as if the devil was chasing them.

And there was Buck, the director of maintenance for the Kade property Jack had met just an hour earlier. His long even strides about to overtake the fleeing duo. Until he paused and raised his shotgun.

"Buck!" Jack bolted out the kitchen door. "Stop!"

Buck paused. Jack watched the lean, six-foot three, subtly graying, brown-haired maintenance director look at him and then back to the terrified camouflage duo. *Did he just grin?*

Buck raised his gun one more time and fired a final shot over the heads of the hefty hunters as they pushed and pulled each other through a fence along the Kade property line.

Jack shoved his own weapon into his waistband and ran up to Buck. He wanted to jerk the gun out of Buck's hands but, decided against it. For several reasons.

"What do you think you're doing?"

Buck was completely calm. He looked Jack up and down, apparently sizing him up. "Poachers. They hop the fence every now and then and I have to chase them off."

"With a gun?"

"They need to know they're not welcome. Otherwise they'll try again."

Jack pinched the bridge of his nose and closed his eyes. He forgot. He was back in Texas.

"Buck, I get it, I do, but I'd rather treat trespassers with a little more caution. You realize you were firing a weapon at two *armed* people who were knowingly committing a crime. They might've shot back."

Buck shrugged. Without a hint of concern. If he believed a person could be bulletproof, he'd be sure Buck was.

He wasn't afraid of Buck though. In fact, he had a sudden respect for the man that he really couldn't rationalize. "Look, I know it's my first day, but the safety of everyone here, including you, is my responsibility. I'm going to add security measures to the entire perimeter of the ranch—those should help us get guys like that arrested if Mr. Kade wants to press charges. Getting arrested would be a pretty good deterrent. Wouldn't it?"

Buck looked him up and down again. Jack was sure he was being judged more on his tone and the way he carried himself than by his words. Buck gave a half-nod of approval, which Jack felt was probably the man's highest form of affirmation. He'd apparently passed some test in Buck's eyes.

Buck leaned his shotgun over his shoulder, his eyes narrowing at Jack. "One more thing,"

"Yes?"

"Since you keep throwing around the word 'ranch' you should know—this place is only called Kade Ranch 'cause Mr. Kade's daddy and granddaddy liked to say, 'meet me back at the ranch.' Like it made them sound like cowboys or somethin'. No Kade has ever owned a single head of cattle." He shook his head. "Shame. It's good land for cattle."

"I see. What about the stables? I guess Mr. Kade rides?"

Buck looked amused. "You'd think so. Yeah, he keeps a few horses. Four right now. But they're just there to entertain guests."

"Interesting."

Buck responded with another half-nod and headed for the garage.

Jack was reasonably confident he and Buck had reached a level of mutual respect. Which was good. Because he was pretty sure he never wanted to be on Buck's bad side.

Walking back in the house, Jack realized no one else appeared rattled by all the gunfire. Buck had no doubt chased off unwelcome visitors in the same manner before.

He decided he needed to introduce himself to more of the house staff. And prayed the rest of his day was uneventful.

It was not.

He found Julie and Mora in the kitchen taking a break from their duties. Julie, he learned, was employed as the upstairs housekeeper and Mora was responsible for all domestic duties on the main floor. Both in their twenties, they were very friendly, very chatty and a little flirtatious.

They were more than happy to give their opinions on different aspects of the ranch and working for Mr. Kade, whom they seemed to genuinely respect. They talked about the swimming pool a lot—that the staff was allowed to use the pool during their off hours when Mr. Kade didn't have guests, and how Jack should join them for a swim soon.

Not wanting to encourage the direction they were steering the conversation, Jack started to cut the meeting short.

"But wait," Julie grabbed his arm, her eyes full of drama, "we have to tell you what happened right here in the kitchen last week!"

And they did.

The two ladies excitedly talked over each other for several minutes detailing a dramatic account of how a frozen corpse fell out of the walk-in freezer in front of the entire staff during breakfast the previous week.

A corpse. A frozen corpse.

What kind of crazy did I sign up for?

Jack was sure Julie and Mora might be the type to exaggerate a story. But you can't just make up something like 'a frozen cadaver fell out of the freezer.'

Jack went looking for Marsten. He wasn't sure what bothered him more, the fact that someone died in the kitchen last week, or that his boss didn't tell him about it. The former was sad, of course, but the latter made his gut clench.

He found Marsten in his study.

"Sir, could I speak with you for a few minutes?" The door was open, but he stood at the doorway until he was invited in.

"Come in, Mr. McKerrick. What can I do for you? Are you getting acquainted with the staff?"

"Yes, sir. That's what I need to discuss with you."

"I don't believe you've met Ms. Green yet." He motioned across the room to a woman retrieving some papers from an antique secretary desk.

Jack hadn't realized there was anyone else in the room. "Oh, I'm sorry. I didn't mean to interrupt."

"Not at all. Mr. McKerrick, this is Ms. Cass Green. Ms. Green is my assistant. She keeps much of my business organized."

Cass Green was slim and attractive and probably several years younger than Marsten, but Jack still couldn't figure out Marsten's age. She wore a well-fitted black sheath dress and her long blonde hair pulled back.

"Nice to meet you Mr. McKerrick. If I can be of any help as you get situated, please let me know." She turned to Mr. Kade. "I'll get this filed for you," she said, indicating the papers she'd retrieved from the desk. She gave Jack a polite smile on her way out.

"Have a seat," Marsten said, indicating one of the leather wingback chairs facing his enormous oak desk.

In every encounter he'd had with his boss so far, Marsten Kade exuded power, intelligence and something else Jack couldn't put his finger on, but Jack always felt he could trust him. In that moment, he found himself desperately hoping he hadn't totally misjudged the man.

"How can I help?"

"Well, sir, per your suggestion, I've been introducing myself to your staff to get a feel for how your residence operates." He paused, willing frustration out of his tone. "I was hoping you could elaborate on some of the stories I'm hearing."

"Certainly. What's concerning you?"

"Sir, you didn't mention that a man was found dead in your kitchen only a week ago." Jack set his jaw and strained to keep his voice professional. But how does someone forget to mention something like that to a newly hired head of security? He was more than a little suspicious that Marsten left that detail out on purpose. He might have made a huge mistake taking this job.

"Ah, yes, of course." Marsten held up both hands as if surrendering. "I'll explain all I can. A most unfortunate accident." He shook his head slowly and Jack scrutinized his somber expression. Possibly sincere.

"He worked for a local nursery and was delivering some plants for Annalee's garden. Have you met Annalee yet?"

"Briefly. She was busy preparing the dinner for this evening, so I told her we could get acquainted later."

"Ah, yes. And I have no doubt you'll soon be very well-acquainted." Marsten smiled. "Annalee is something of an unofficial mother hen to everyone here. She makes everyone's business her concern, but she's so likeable no one seems to mind. And a word of warning, her hobby is matchmaking, so if you already have a girlfriend, best to let her know that up front. She'll probably ask you that before you get a chance to tell her, but be forewarned, she can be persistent."

Ok, good to know, but what he really wanted to know is why there had been a dead body in the kitchen. "Understood. But if you don't mind, sir, the corpse? Could you please explain?"

"Yes, yes of course. Annalee was on her way out to run an errand when he, the plant delivery man, showed up. She said she called out to him that he was welcome to help himself to a pitcher of tea in the kitchen, and she left."

"But how did he end up in the freezer? You said it was an accident."

"Yes, that's what the police decided. Annalee didn't open the freezer until almost twenty-four hours later...so, he didn't make it. Apparently, the safety latch on the inside in broken. I have no idea why he walked into the freezer after Annalee left, but I can't say I'm totally shocked either."

"Why not?"

"Well, sometimes when people come here, if they're left alone, they like to wander around. An enormous, old mansion. People get curious, you know?"

"Yes, I can understand the curiosity factor, but to walk into the freezer? Seems like a strange thing to do."

"I agree. But the police couldn't find any evidence that it was anything more than an accident." He was shaking his head again. "Of course, they really didn't have anything to work with. I felt terrible that none of the security cameras were on around the kitchen that morning. That was after I let my previous head of security go. I think the fact that they couldn't find a single connection between the poor man and anyone here, besides the fact that he delivered plants that morning, was the main reason they decided it must have been an accident. Not a soul here knew him."

"I see." Jack didn't feel much better. The explanation was strange, but plausible. It still bugged him that Marsten hadn't mentioned the death earlier. He stood to leave.

"Thank you for your time, sir."

"Of course. And if my staff or I can help you in any way with your transition into this position, please don't hesitate to ask."

Jack looked his boss in the eye. Marsten Kade seemed genuine and mysterious all at once. He would be a tough guy to figure out.

"Thank you, sir." Jack left the study wondering what he'd gotten himself into.

Meeting the staff over the course of his first day helped Jack get a better feel for Marsten Kade. It hadn't made sense to him that a billionaire like Kade would hire someone he'd only heard a couple of war stories about to provide security instead of hiring a company with an established reputation. That is, until he'd met the rest of the staff at Kade Ranch. None of them had applied to work for Marsten Kade. Each employee had been acquired under unique, and sometimes vague, circumstances. He wasn't sure how he felt about that. But what did he know? Maybe that's how billionaires did things.

After three days of familiarizing himself with some of the staff he had a few take-aways—Buck was a man of action, but few words. And tough as nails. Annalee floated somewhere in between doting grandmother and fairy godmother. And Felix, the IT expert, possessed a level of skill that would have most likely landed him at the NSA—or prison. But instead, here he was, working for Marsten Kade. Jack was sure there was a story there.

He still needed to get to know Mora and Julie better, without encouraging their flirting. And there was Cody, the young chauffer. And Cass Green, Marsten's assistant. He hadn't had the chance to talk to them much yet.

Motion in the hospital hallway pulled Jack back to the present. Marsten and Brynnan were ready to leave.

Half an hour later they were pulling up to Brynnan's parents' house, where she'd been staying temporarily. It was a nice home, but it was no multi-million-dollar mansion—the Marshes and the Kades lived differently. Lifestyles and bank accounts were completely irrelevant that night. Pain and loss do not discriminate.

Jack watched heartbreak weigh heavily on his boss throughout the evening. Marsten was obviously very close to his half-brother and sister-in-law. He felt for the man.

What he didn't expect, was that his boss's suffering didn't trouble him near as much as Brynnan's. She'd lost both her parents. In one night. Without warning. He was close to his own family, despite the deployments, and couldn't imagine the sorrow she must be experiencing.

He was surprised, and uncomfortable, at how quickly her teary eyes evoked an intense instinct to comfort her. An urge to wrap his arm around her. A compulsion to protect her—from what, he didn't know. He couldn't do anything about her tragic loss. But her tears were slicing through him.

Admirably, she was neither despondent or hysterical. On the contrary, her depth of courage seemed greater than her depth of sadness. She was heartbroken, of course, but she obviously possessed a strong willingness to put one foot in front of the other throughout her bouts with grief that evening.

He was relieved Marsten was so attentive to her. That made it easier for Jack to keep his distance, remain alert. Not that he would've ever considered acting less than professional, he was just glad someone was comforting Brynnan. Because having to stand sentry and watch her mourn alone, would have been torture. *Torture? Her feelings really shouldn't affect him that much.*

He told himself he was only feeling compassion for a fellow human being. Yep. That's it. Compassion.

Although he was beginning to feel the threat level to his boss was minimal—the emailed threats sent to Marsten were probably all bark and no bite—he still felt it would be prudent to walk the perimeter of the house every hour. Whether it was overkill or not, it was his job. Besides, it gave him something to do.

When he reentered the house after his second uneventful security sweep, Brynnan was waiting for him.

She looked emotionally and physically exhausted, but she was trying to force a smile. "Hi. All quiet out there, I assume?"

"Yes, very." She probably thought he was crazy to patrol the yard. The Marshes obviously didn't have hired security, so she wasn't accustomed to someone monitoring her parents' rosebushes for threats.

If she thought he was crazy, she was being gracious. She forced a smile again.

"We decided to order a pizza. I never ate dinner tonight. Marsten said y'all haven't eaten either. What kind of pizza would you like?"

He was relieved to see her eyes regaining some confidence. "Oh, anything. Thanks."

She squinted at him. "I think you're just being polite. You probably have a preference."

He couldn't believe she was actually making

him smile. Yes, she was still hurting, probably would be for a long time, but Brynnan Marsh was going to be okay.

"Alright," he said. "No anchovies. Other than that, I'll eat anything."

He was sure her eyes, beautiful eyes, smiled at him. Though the rest of her face was still too drained to cooperate.

"You don't know what you're agreeing to. I normally order cauliflower crust, light cheese and veggies. If you want pepperoni or something, you better speak up."

"Actually, that sounds great." He wasn't lying. He worked out a lot, so he ate a lot, but he preferred eating healthier meals. Greasy tasted good ten years ago. Not anymore.

She squinted at him, again, as if she wasn't sure if he was just trying to be agreeable or not. "Okay, I'll put in the order. It will probably be thirty minutes."

"Sounds good. Thanks."

She gave a quick nod and was gone again. He watched her leave and realized he was still smiling. And the room was warmer. Or at least he was.

Oh, no.

What is wrong with you, man? Get it together. Brynnan was his boss's grieving niece. Being attracted to her tonight was all kinds of wrong. For so many reasons.

So. Many. Reasons.

He'd tried dating again, about a year after he'd been held captive. And that experience taught him he wasn't what any woman needed. Not now, and maybe not ever.

He'd been taken prisoner after a mission went horribly wrong. At least he was the only one captured. He protected his men. They made it out. He, however, spent two weeks in enemy hands. His mental, emotional and spiritual perseverance was tested to an excruciating degree before he was rescued.

He came back to the states for a while, completed all the mandatory physical and mental evals required, and returned to active duty as soon as they allowed him. He wanted to keep moving on. He didn't want his time in captivity to steal even more of his life from him. But it had—there were still lingering repercussions whether he acknowledged them or not.

He'd been overconfident. He met Heather at a charity chili cook-off. She was smart, sweet, and kind. But a few dates later, he fell asleep on her couch during a movie, and had one of his nightmares—one of those lingering repercussions.

He hadn't told her he'd been held captive. That night, he had to explain everything. His nightmare frightened her. His explanation horrified her. She looked at him like he was broken—and completely irreparable.

She didn't say much when she broke things off, but the fact that he was hopeless relationship material rang loud and clear.

So, no, he wasn't going to let his thoughts about Brynnan Marsh stray from anything but completely professional.

I need to get my head straight—maybe some fresh air. It was a little early to go on another check of the perimeter, but maybe he would anyway.

His phone buzzed. It was Felix, the resourceful, albeit shady, IT genius. He reported the threatening emails were traced to a guy notorious for similar stunts. Apparently, he'd sent angry messages to dozens of wealthy people over the years. Never carried out a threat. Yep, all bark and no bite. Well, that's one piece of good news.

A loud beep, followed by a computerized voice, echoed through the house, "Back door. Open."

The Marshes security system. Why would Marsten or Brynnan open the back door?

Brynnan entered the living area from the kitchen, surprised to see Jack with his face tense, his stance intentional.

"Did your uncle go out the back door?" he whispered.

"No, he's upstairs. I thought you—"

Jack held his fingers to his lips for her to be quiet. Ok, this is not good. His level of alertness stopped her. Froze her. A soft thud sounded. She wasn't sure what it was, but it didn't come from upstairs. *Someone else is in the house.*

Faster than she could process his movements, Jack rushed to her and pulled her to the ground behind the sofa. His strong form was halfway on top of her when she heard the first shots. Then glass breaking.

Jack readjusted himself off of her a bit. She could breathe better, but she was wedged between the back of the sofa and his chest. More shots. Jack was firing around the corner of the sofa now. She wanted to cover her ears, but her arms were pinned. The gunfire was so loud. So. Loud. She squeezed her eyes shut as if it would help. It did not.

Terrified of distracting Jack as he discharged his weapon over and over, she swallowed her scream, held her breath. His hard chest was shoved against her face with so much force she could feel the buttons on his dress shirt pressing into her cheek. It wasn't comfortable. But she did feel well shielded by the mass of muscle on top of her—a mass of muscle and strength that apparently knew what he was doing.

Not complaining.

The gunfire stopped, and a heavy silence hung over them. She was still too scared to move. Or breathe.

Jack shifted away a few inches. "Stay here," he whispered, so closely she felt his warm breath on her cheek.

She didn't have the ability to nod yet, but she had no intention of going anywhere. Apparently, he realized as much. He got to his feet and slowly walked around the sofa. She waited a few seconds, listening to her heart thundering in her ears.

The exchange of gunfire had lasted only seconds, but she was afraid it would take much longer for her hearing to return to normal.

"Brynnan! Brynnan!" It was her uncle, yelling from the top of the stairs.

"Don't come down, Mr. Kade." Jack's voice was confident and calm. "She's fine. But the shooter is at the foot of the stairs. He's alive, but unconscious. I don't want to move him before the medics get here. If you'll call an ambulance, I'll check on Miss Marsh."

"Are you sure he's..."

"He's not a threat, sir. I took his weapon. And

restrained him, in case he regains consciousness. I cleared the house between here and the back door. If he wasn't alone, I would've seen an accomplice."

"I'll call 911, you see to Brynnan."

"Yes, sir."

Brynnan heard Jack's footsteps return to her spot behind the sofa. He knelt down beside her.

"It's alright. Are you hurt?"

She wanted to sit up and say 'No, I'm just fine,' but her body wouldn't cooperate.

Intense brown eyes, radiating with worry, looked her over, assessing for injuries.

"I'm... I'm okay." Her voice betrayed her. She wished she sounded stronger.

He took her hand and helped her to her feet. Instinctively, she started to turn in the direction of all the chaos just moments before, but he grabbed her shoulders and kept her back to the injured shooter.

"Don't look," he said quietly. "Are you sure you're okay?"

She finally met his gaze. The concern storming in his eyes coaxed a nod from her, but she was trembling uncontrollably. And he noticed. He pulled her to him and wrapped her in his strong arms as if it was the most natural reflex to her panicked reaction.

She was embarrassed and relieved at the same time.

She'd met this man only hours ago, but his embrace calmed her like nothing she'd ever experienced. He rubbed her back and her breathing started to regulate.

"Thank you," she whispered into his chest.

He eased back just enough to look into her

face. He tucked some stray hairs behind her ear. "You're safe. The police will be here soon. Will you wait in the kitchen, away from...all this?"

"Yeah, okay."

He guided her to the kitchen with his hand on the small of her back. She took her first deep breath when she reached the refrigerator. Maybe she should get some water.

"Stay in here. I'll be right back," he said.

"Wait, where are you going?" She may have felt the teeniest bit terrified for him to leave her alone at that moment.

"If you're okay in here, I need to check on the shooter and assess his injuries."

"Okay," she nodded. He obviously expected her to stay put, but when he walked out of the kitchen, she was right on his heels.

Before he could get the words out to tell her to go back, she was staring at the bloody stranger crumpled on the floor.

"I... I have a first aid kit," she said.

He turned to her, surprise and concern on his face. "That would be helpful. But you don't need to be here. Leave the first aid kit on the kitchen counter, I'll get it in a minute." He knelt by the shooter and put pressure on his wound with a dish cloth he grabbed in the kitchen.

Marsten appeared on the stairs, close enough to take in the whole scene.

"Sir, do you recognize him?" Jack asked.

"No, no I certainly don't. The police and an ambulance are on the way. Thank you, Jack."

Jack responded with a nod.

Marsten maneuvered himself from the

bottom step. "I can step over him without touching him. Brynnan and I will wait for the police at the front."

"Okay but, stay inside. I'm almost certain he's alone, but I haven't cleared the block. He's losing blood. I need to stay with him." said Jack.

Marsten assured him he understood. "Brynnan, come wait with me in the living room."

"I'm going to get the first aid kit first. I'll be there in a minute."

She darted back to the kitchen and threw open cabinets until she eyed the large, red box her mother had recently purchased, 'just in case.' She pushed her mother's smiling image from her mind, before it had time to derail her emotions. Grabbing the box, she ran back to Jack, knelt beside him, and opened the kit.

His eyebrows shot up at her presence. "Miss Marsh, I've got this. Stay with your uncle."

"I want to help," she said, ripping open a package of gauze. There was so much blood. She'd seen more though. So much more. This guy might have a chance. "Here." She handed him the gauze and started digging through the kit to see what else they could possibly use.

It sounded crazy, even to her, that she felt as safe as she did at the moment. She had every reason to dissolve into hysterics. After everything she'd been through in her past, tonight's events should have unraveled her. And forced her into the fetal position.

But for some inexplicable reason, she felt safe next to this...this...*what did Marsten call him?* Well, whatever his title was, he was good at his job.

And she felt more comfortable *doing*

something, than standing around waiting. Maybe if she kept searching through the kit for bandages her hands would stop shaking. Or maybe she was just distracting herself from processing what had just happened. Or why.

She felt Jack's narrowed gaze. He was definitely more worried about her than their 'patient.' But their 'patient' had just tried to kill him, so maybe that was excusable.

She watched him hold pressure on the wound. Surely this wasn't a common scenario for her uncle's employee, but he showed no doubt, or hesitation, about how to attend to a gunshot wound. Like he'd done it before.

He looked like he wanted to say something, but his mouth simply held a grim line. His eyes kept darting across the bloody shooter to her face, concern all over his handsome features. *Handsome?* Was she seriously thinking that? This had to be the most inappropriate time to notice someone was attractive. What was wrong with her? Not that it wasn't true. Thick dark hair, strong jaw, broad shoulders, and the kindest eyes she'd ever... But good grief, her attention needed to be on the bleeding man who tried to kill them just minutes ago.

Tried to kill them.

Images from the past spun through her brain, making her dizzy. *Never mind. Go ahead and think about how attractive this guy is—anything to keep from passing out from fear.*

Sirens blared outside. Thank goodness.

Everything after that was a blur.

She realized she'd been on an adrenaline rush when it completely evaporated. She was beyond exhausted. She talked to the police, answered their questions. For the second time that evening. Would this day ever end?

By the time the police finally left, her body felt heavy, her mind dazed. She felt so drained she didn't think she could make it up the stairs to her room. Nope. That wasn't happening. Did her uncle just ask her something? Everything sounded distant. Her thoughts blurred. Suddenly, Jack filled her vision. He was saying something about moving them to a hotel.

"No, no," she said. Not a hotel. But she wasn't sure if she said that out loud.

She heard the words, "going into shock." Something firm broke her fall, and everything went black.

A voice coaxed her eyes to open, but nothing came into focus.

"Miss Marsh, can you hear me? I think she's waking up, sir."

Where was she? Who was talking? Panic coursed through her. She remembered shooting. And blood. The hospital. Her parents...maybe it was a dream. She bolted up or, tried to at least.

"Whoa. Miss Marsh, take it easy. You passed out. Rest for a few minutes."

The voice belonged to the worried eyes and strong arms trying to guide her back down on the sofa.

She leaned back on the cushions and massaged her temples. Reality came rushing back.

None of it had been a dream. Her parents...the shooter...

Her parents were really gone. Her relationship with them wouldn't get the second chance she hoped for. Her eyes stung.

And the man with the gun...was he coming for her? A repeat of the past?

She'd tamped down the fear—and all the what-ifs—while the police were questioning her. But she was so exhausted. Her brave façade was dangerously close to crumbling. *Oh, for crying out loud*—she'd passed out, *that* probably constitutes the end of her I've-got-it-together charade.

"I'll get her some water," said Marsten.

Her mind retreated to the repeated council from years ago... 'concentrate on slow, deep breaths...slow, deep breaths...slow, deep breaths...'

She felt a warm presence beside her.

Jack softly rubbed her arm. "You okay?"

She nodded mechanically. His touch gently pulled her to her senses.

"Yes, I'm sorry. I—"

"Don't apologize. You need to rest."

His deep, brown eyes were so kind, she thought she could get lost in them. But as that thought flashed in her mind, he suddenly stood and cleared his throat.

"Your uncle hopes you'll consider staying in a hotel tonight. There's damage to the back door—"

Marsten returned and handed her a glass of ice water. "Yes, sweetheart, it would be safer. I made some arrangements while you were talking to the police earlier. I've reserved a suite at the Driskill."

"Is that really necessary? I don't see how

anything else could possibly happen tonight. I just want to go to bed. A hotel really wouldn't make me feel any—"

A jolt of realization on Marsten's face stopped her short. She knew what he was thinking. A hotel wasn't going to make her feel safer.

Being in a hotel hadn't kept her safe in the past. She'd rather be in the house, with the alarm set. It was the security alarm that alerted them to the shooter tonight. She wouldn't have an alarm in a hotel room. And apparently, hotel room doors weren't that difficult to breach.

Marsten seemed to be reading her mind. He looked like he made a decision and plastered a smile on his face. "Very well. We'll stay here tonight. Jack and I will be here with you. You get some rest."

"Thank you," she answered quietly. She was more thankful they were staying than she could voice. If she had to be alone in her parents' empty house tonight, the silence would overwhelm her.

They ate some of the pizza, now cold, left by a very confused delivery guy earlier. Apparently, it was his first experience delivering pizza to a crime scene.

After a little sustenance, Brynnan felt she had just enough energy to drag herself to her bedroom. She said goodnight to her uncle and Jack and forced her legs to climb the stairs.

Too tired for her nightly routine, she collapsed on the bed, her body begging for sleep. But her mind showed no mercy. Her thoughts held her captive, forcing her to relive the phone call, the hospital, the gunfire...

Alone, and weak from hours of stifling the bulk of her despair, she submitted to the waves of emotion crashing over her. Sobs racked her body. She clung to her pillow like a life preserver in a storm, praying she wouldn't drown in her grief and fear. Suppressed memories of violence pulled themselves from the dark places, and fought for position, front and center, in her mind. If Jack hadn't intervened tonight...

She tried to pray, but, like in the hospital, all she could manage was, *"Help me, God."*

She knew God was there. Knew He heard her. But she was going to need a tremendous dose of comfort and strength to be able to sleep tonight. And face tomorrow.

She repeated her short cry for help to the Lord and a verse blanketed her consciousness. *"So do not fear, for I am with you; do not be dismayed, for I am your God. I will strengthen you and help you; I will uphold you with my righteous right hand."*

She clenched the pillow in a death grip, as if needing to squeeze the scripture into her palms to keep it from floating away.

But the truth wasn't going anywhere.

God was watching over her. Whether she understood any of the chaos or not.

The last conscious thought she had before sleep overtook her was of Jack. Maybe God sent someone to keep her safe this time...

Jack threw away the pizza box and was relieved to find a Keurig on the counter. Caffeine was a good idea. He wouldn't be sleeping tonight.

He didn't like coincidences. It didn't sit right

with him that an armed man would descend on the Marshes' home the same night they died, just after Marsten Kade arrives. He didn't know if the intruder had something to do with the Marshes, or with his boss, but he couldn't accept that the break-in was completely random.

He eyed his boss, still leaning against the kitchen counter, appearing lost in his thoughts.

"Sir, you should get some rest. I'm staying up, just in case, but it should stay quiet tonight."

Marsten had an uneasy look. Again. He tried to rationalize his suspicions earlier, but now, Jack couldn't shake the sick feeling his boss knew more than he'd told the police. Working for Marsten Kade might not be nearly as boring as he feared, but he couldn't stay in this position if his boss was involved in anything illegal. He needed to broach the subject carefully.

"Sir, you said earlier you didn't recognize the intruder, but sometimes people can recall things after the adrenaline settles. Do you have any idea who he might be?"

Marsten looked at Jack with knowing eyes, and a bit of admiration. "I knew I hired the right man. You're smart, Jack, that's what I was looking for."

Not the response he was expecting. What on earth had he gotten himself into? *God, please give me wisdom on how to navigate this.*

"Okay. Thank you, sir, but what do you know about this guy?"

Marsten sighed and sat down in one of the kitchen chairs, apparently trying to organize his thoughts. Jack sat down across from him.

Marsten leaned in, fixing his gaze on Jack.

"You think I wasn't honest earlier? I was. I didn't recognize that man. However," he said, rubbing a hand across his tired face, and keeping his voice low, "I can't help but have suspicions."

"You think the shooter was coming after you? You think he was one of the people emailing threats? I heard from Felix earlier, I really don't think we need to be concerned about those emails. Just some misguided individual blowing off steam."

"I'm glad to hear that. I was hoping the emails were empty threats," Marsten said, without looking any less concerned. He wasn't worried about the emails.

"What else do you suspect, sir?"

Marsten gave an uneasy nod. His eyes softened.

"There's something you need to know."

Jack didn't like the sound of that. "Sir?"

"I'm desperately hoping Jonathan and Rachel's accident and the attack tonight are both completely unrelated, but..."

This definitely sounded bad. Now he *knew* Marsten hadn't been forthcoming earlier. How was he supposed to do his job with his boss keeping things from him?

"Sir, if there's anything at all you can tell me that could help me keep you safe, please, tell me everything."

Pain etched deep lines on Marsten's face. But he wasn't a weak man. He took a strengthening breath and began his explanation. "Like I said, I'm hoping none of it is connected, but...Brynnan was kidnapped several years ago."

The news nearly knocked the breath out of

Jack. He'd witnessed worse. Much worse. But picturing Brynnan as the victim…something inside him twisted painfully.

"How long ago? Who was it?"

Jack saw deep sadness in his boss' eyes, but his voice was all business. "Actually, there were two incidents. She was taken from her home when she was sixteen. She was held for thirty-six hours before the FBI found her in a warehouse. Then, when she was eighteen, she was held hostage at a hotel for almost three days."

Jack could tell there was more to this story. "The two incidents were related?"

"Yes, and no." Marsten sighed. "You need to know, Rachel, Brynnan's mother, is…" he stopped himself, then painfully continued, "*was* the daughter of Bobby Alesi."

"Should I know that name?"

"Not necessarily. The criminals you're accustom to chasing travel in different circles than Alesi. But your father, he's FBI, isn't he?"

Jack never told Marsten his father's occupation, but he already assumed he knew. He had the feeling he'd been thoroughly vetted before his hire.

"Yes, he is."

Marsten nodded. "If he doesn't know who Alesi is, he knows people who do. I'm sure of that. Alesi, his brothers, and his son, run a significant percentage of the organized crime on the west coast."

Jack needed to process this. But he had several questions first. "Are you saying Alesi took Ms. Marsh? Why?"

"No, it wasn't him, his enemies. Family is

35

important to Alesi. His enemies know that. Rachel was always traveling, always abroad with Jonathan at her side. Brynnan was so young…" Emotion gripped his voice, prohibiting him from voicing the rest of his thought. He cleared his throat, composed himself and continued. "On both occasions, when she was sixteen and eighteen, a rival of Alesi's used Brynnan as leverage."

"The same rival both times?"

"No, two different ones." He let out a haggard sigh. "So, you see, too many people, too many of the *wrong* people, know Brynnan is Bobby Alesi's granddaughter. I don't know if what happened tonight is related or not, but I thought you should know."

"You think someone could have killed Rachel *intentionally*, to hurt Alesi? Or went after Ms. Marsh tonight for the same reason?"

Marsten's eyes dimmed, clouded with dark grief. "Possibly," he whispered.

Jack's head was spinning. Marsten Kade's surprises weren't going to stop. He needed to accept that. If he wanted the simple security detail he assumed this job was, he needed to walk out now and not look back. Because there wasn't anything simple about Marsten Kade's life.

But he wasn't walking out. Not now and not anytime soon. Marsten frustrated him to a degree, and Jack was wary of skeletons that were possibly in Marsten Kade's closet, but for reasons he couldn't articulate, he trusted the man.

Jack blew out a long breath. "Thank you for telling me, sir. The police said they would let me know what they could after questioning the intruder.

If anything points to organized crime on the west coast, I'll loop them in." He raked a hand through his hair, not believing he was about to utter his next words. "And I'll do what I can to see if the FBI has picked up any chatter about enemies of Alesi targeting his family recently."

Jack wasn't naive. He now realized his connection to the FBI was one reason he'd been offered his position. But Marsten was assuming a lot. Surely, he didn't expect Jack to have much clout with the FBI, did he? Yes, he would ask his dad about Alesi, and *maybe*, his dad could ask around about relevant chatter, but that was a presumptive 'maybe.'

"Thank you, Jack."

Jack gave a nod. "Please get some rest, sir. I'll see you in the morning."

Jack wouldn't need coffee to keep him up tonight. Marsten's bombshell about Brynnan's grandfather, and her past, would keep him wired till dawn.

It was impossible to remove Brynnan's face from his mind. She'd made such a striking and innocent impression on him...the idea of her having been kidnapped, *twice* no less... Bile rose in his throat.

If the intruder, whose blood was still on his shirt, survived his injuries, the police would question him. But they wouldn't be sharing much information with Jack—being Marsten Kade's head of security wasn't going to grant him privileges with law enforcement. And he needed to know everything. His boss needed to know what kind of danger Brynnan was in, if any, and he could tell Marsten desperately wanted to know if Jonathan and Rachel's deaths were purely accidental. Or something else.

He rubbed the back of his neck. He couldn't believe he was going to be asking his dad for information.

Jack and his dad shared a great mutual respect for one another's careers. The FBI and Special Forces operated in different spheres, but with a similar mission. Within each, they fought evil and protected the innocent. Their respective callings provided a camaraderie beyond the typical bond of father and son.

He'd never collaborated *with* his father on anything though. Asking him for FBI intelligence would be a new one.

His mind wandered back to Brynnan and how best to keep her safe. *But wait, what are the parameters of this?* His job was to protect Marsten. He assumed that translated to protecting his niece while they were in the same house, but what about after tonight? Would Marsten want to return to his ranch tomorrow, or the next day? If so, could Jack leave Brynnan in Austin knowing what he knew—the danger she could be in? Depending on what Jack could find out from the FBI, Brynnan might need a constant security detail.

Her innocent eyes flashed through his mind. And an urge to protect her swelled within him.

He shoved a hand through his hair, blowing out a long breath.

Deciding he could use some of the long night ahead to wash the shooter's blood from his clothes, he started unbuttoning his shirt. Brynnan didn't need another reminder of the incident in the morning.

Maybe he was getting ahead of himself. Maybe the police or FBI would give them some good news tomorrow. Maybe the car accident, the intruder, and Brynnan's past had nothing to do with each other.

Maybe.

But he doubted it.

Brynnan would stay safe tonight, though. That much he could guarantee.

So as not to wake Brynnan the next morning, Jack rifled through the kitchen cabinets looking for Keurig pods as quietly as possible. He hadn't needed much caffeine last night, but his body was demanding coffee this morning. And waffles. But he'd settle for coffee.

"Good morning, Jack. What are you doing?" asked Marsten, sounding more upbeat than Jack had expected.

"Just looking for..." He finally found a drawer full of dark roast K-cups. Small victories. "Would you like some coffee sir?"

"Yes, thank you." Marsten squinted at the bright turquoise Keurig on the counter. "You know how to work that contraption?"

"Um, yes. I don't know how to use an espresso machine, but yes, I can handle a Keurig." Was he serious? It wasn't rocket science.

Marsten shrugged. "Annalee bought one once. For me to use on her days off. I tried. Somehow, I broke it." He shrugged again.

He *was* serious. Wow. Well, Jack shouldn't judge. He could make coffee. And bake a frozen pizza. But it wasn't like he had mad skills in the kitchen.

Marsten accepted a cup of coffee and sat down at the breakfast bar. He gave Jack a pointed look. Something was up.

"I have news," Marsten said.

Oh, boy. What now? He gave his boss his undivided attention.

Marsten sat his mug down. "I've been talking to Brynnan this morning. I've convinced her to come back to the ranch with us, after the funeral, to stay a while. She's being very brave about all this, but... Well, I know she's fully grown, and perfectly capable..." He apparently didn't know how to finish his thought. "In any case, she's agreed to come stay at the ranch until her condo is ready in College Station."

"In College Station?"

"Yes, she's supposed to start a new position at A&M in the fall. She purchased a new condo, but it won't be completed until August. She planned to live with her parents for the summer..." He just left it there. Likely, living in this empty house for the summer wasn't appealing to her now. And after last night, he wasn't sure it was even safe.

Marsten looked toward the hallway, presumedly, to make sure Brynnan wasn't about to walk in on their conversation. She wasn't. He lowered his voice anyway. "Jack, I know she wouldn't want me to, but I feel responsible for her. With Jonathan and Rachel gone, and the intruder, and... well, I'm just informing you that she's your top priority for now."

Jack started to say something, but Marsten held up a hand. "I know you're still figuring out how to do your job, and I know I'm throwing this on top of everything, but we play the hand we're dealt, right? Besides, you're hiring more men for your security team, correct?"

"Yes, sir, they should start arriving this week."

"Excellent. Hire as many men as you think you need."

Jack may have let his surprise show on his face.

"I trust you. Hire a team. A team of people you trust. You can keep the ranch, *and* me, *and* Brynnan safe. I'm sure of it."

"Thank you for your confidence. You'll have my best, sir."

Marsten's phone buzzed. He nodded to Jack and walked into the living room to take the call.

Jack's head was spinning. Again. Why did Marsten trust him so much? What on earth had his military buddies said to the man? He acted like Jack could walk on water.

And now he was responsible for Brynnan's safety. An unfamiliar stress sat like a rock in his gut. He'd had more difficult assignments in the military, of course, but the people assigning those missions had access to the most comprehensive intelligence on the planet, and he was working with a team of elite operators.

Now, it was just him.

Protecting a sweet, beautiful...um, protecting his boss's niece, the granddaughter of a notorious mobster.

He pinched the bridge of his nose and closed his eyes. *This is what I get for praying this job wouldn't be boring.*

The nagging feeling from last night was back. He hoped he was overreacting. He needed to talk to his dad, ASAP. Brynnan was still upstairs, so now was as good a time as any.

His dad answered on the second ring. "Hey, son, how's the new job going?"

No easy way to answer that question. "Interesting, so far. Listen, I actually have a favor to ask. A big favor."

"Okay, what's up?" His dad's tone conveyed he read the seriousness in Jack's statement.

"Could you find out if there's been any recent chatter in Texas referencing Bobby Alesi?"

"Bobby Alesi?"

"You know the name?"

"Yes, I do. Jack, what's going on?"

He didn't miss the concern in his father's words.

Jack filled him in on the events of the last eighteen hours. And everything Marsten revealed. His dad didn't respond immediately.

"Dad?"

"I'm here. I thought this was going to be a less stressful job for you. Your mother was hoping your career change would mean you wouldn't get shot at."

Jack almost grinned. "I know. This isn't what I thought it would be. But I want to see it through for now. I'm worried about Mr. Kade and his niece. I need to find out what's going on."

"Agreed. I'll see what I can do."

"Thanks. I'll be in touch."

"And Jack..."

"Yes?"

"Be careful."

Yep, his Dad was worried. Not a good sign. This Alesi guy was probably very bad news.

"Will do."

"Alright, talk to you soon."

"Thanks, Dad. Bye."

CHAPTER THREE

For the next two days, Jack followed on the heels of Marsten and Brynnan, while they made funeral arrangements, and accepted food, flowers and visitors.

Brynnan amazed him. She navigated every conversation and attended to each task with exceptional grace. He'd wanted, so many times, to say something to her. To offer some encouragement. But he wasn't sure what was appropriate. They'd just met. And he was here solely as security. Her uncle's employee.

At least he was successfully ignoring how beautiful her eyes were. Yep. Not noticing the pull those innocent, warm eyes had on him. Not at all.

He shifted every other minute from feeling he was hovering too much or too little. He needed to let this family mourn in privacy, but he needed to be on high-alert and present if another threat surfaced.

And nothing he'd learned over that forty-eight

hours had given him reason to relax.

He talked to the officers who responded to Jonathan and Rachel's accident. Her parents had been forced off the road by a dark colored Audi. No arrest yet. They were still sifting through traffic cam footage from that night to try to get a license plate number.

The gunman was still in the hospital. He was awake. But the only word he spoke to the officers who tried to question him was 'lawyer.' The officers did share that when they realized he wasn't going to talk, and were about to leave, the guy's lawyer walked right in the hospital room. That really piqued Jack's interest. He was pretty sure the average burglar didn't have a lawyer on retainer.

None of it sat well with Jack.

His dad had texted a couple of times. He didn't have much intel yet, but he had a couple of friends he expected to hear back from. Hopefully soon.

He was thankful for the close relationship he had with his dad. Their only arguments were about college football rankings. Every. Single. Fall. But, other than that, they got along, respected each other. His father was extremely professional, as was Jack. They'd never shared any confidential information, and he hoped his dad wouldn't see his recent request as crossing a line. Jack didn't believe it was. Because what mattered was keeping Brynnan safe. And Marsten. Though Jack had a terrible feeling Brynnan Marsh was in more danger than her uncle.

Surely the FBI wouldn't argue the need to do everything possible to keep Brynnan safe. He just hoped they agreed that sharing intel with him served a common interest.

The funeral came and went. Everyone said it was nice. Brynnan supposed it was. She knew both her parents had a saving relationship with Jesus, so there was plenty of hope and encouragement in the brief service. She was glad when it was over though.

She was ready to leave Austin. She had no idea if she was going to feel comfortable staying at her uncle's home—she didn't want to be a burden, and she'd never visited there before. But she was definitely ready to leave her parents' empty house.

After she finished packing, she walked through the house one last time, double checked that the refrigerator was cleaned out, and made sure the back door, recently repaired, was securely locked. She tested the knob and turned to leave, bumping right into a wall of muscle. She let out a squeaky gasp. Embarrassing.

"I'm sorry," said Jack. "I... I didn't mean to startle you." He backed up, out of her personal space.

Why did he look embarrassed? She was the one not paying attention.

"I was going to check the back door, but I see you beat me to it," he said.

He looked more comfortable now. His easy smile made her feel less self-conscious about her less-than-eloquent squeal a moment ago. "Yeah. All locked up. Is Marsten ready to leave?"

"Yes, in a couple of minutes. Cody arrived a few minutes ago, and he and I put all the bags you had sitting by the front door in your car. Is there anything else you need?"

They loaded the car for her? They didn't need to do that. Wait—"Cody? Who's Cody?"

A hint of confusion darted across his features. Handsome features. Oh, good grief, she needed to stop looking at him like that. Ignoring his thick brown hair and warm brown eyes would be so much easier if he wasn't so considerate to her all the time. But it was his kindness she appreciated the most over the past few days. She was starting to step out of the fog of grief she'd been in. And she was realizing the face that belonged to all that gentle compassion was a very handsome face. She really needed to stop thinking that way though. No way a guy like this needed all her issues in his life.

She still had no idea why her uncle had brought security with him. She hadn't felt like asking. But after the break-in on the first night, she realized she was able to sleep better knowing Jack was in the house.

"Um, Cody is your uncle's chauffer. He looks barely twenty years old, but he's a nice guy, and your uncle has a lot of confidence in him. I'm sorry, I assumed you knew him."

Chauffer? She started to laugh. But noted the lack of sarcasm in his tone. *What?*

"Chauffer? Marsten has a chauffeur? Why?"

Now the confusion that flew across his face a moment ago registered in cement. He opened his mouth and closed it again without saying anything. Apparently, she'd asked a difficult question.

"Since neither of you planned on leaving the house the past few days, except for the two trips to the funeral home, he didn't think it necessary for Cody to bring his car to Austin. But since you want to take your car to the ranch, and it's packed full, we'll need two cars to get back."

She was still confused. "But where's the car you came in on the first night?" She hadn't thought about it until now. She hadn't seen Marsten's car in the driveway. Wow, that fog of grief she'd been stumbling around in had been thicker than she'd thought. What else hadn't she noticed?

"We took his helicopter from the ranch to the hospital. Then we brought you back here in an Uber because Marsten didn't think you felt up to driving. Remember? The next day I took an Uber to pick up your car." He spoke the words so gently. He obviously realized she'd been so distracted... Wait. *His helicopter?*

"His helicopter? He has a helicopter?"

He stared at her for a few beats, but she couldn't interpret everything in his expression. And there was a lot.

Finally, he dropped the formal professionalism. His eyes held hers. What was that? Sympathy? Concern?

He popped his head into the hallway, apparently checking that Marsten wasn't nearby, then moved all the way back into the mudroom, closer this time, into her personal space. He kept his voice to a low whisper.

"Have you ever visited his ranch? Or his home in Houston?"

"No," she shook her head. "He always visited us. Why are we whispering?" This was weird. Was something wrong? Was going to her uncle's ranch a bad idea? Why?

"So, you didn't know the ranch is actually a country estate with a mansion, several guest houses, a house staff..."

She knew her eyes were bugging out. No. No, she didn't know Marsten had a... a *house staff?* She shook her head again. "Um, no. All that is his? And a helicopter?"

Jack nodded.

"So, he's wealthy?"

Jack stared at her. Wow. How did she not know? Brynnan and Marsten had seemed so close the past few days. What was going on? Why hadn't Marsten told her? And why hadn't Marsten told *him* that she didn't know? She was obviously about to find out anyway. They were minutes from driving to the ranch.

"Yeah, you could say that." He looked back to the hallway and strained his ears. Marsten was on a call upstairs. He could hear his muffled voice. What should he say to her? She looked so confused. He realized over the past few days she was not accustomed to living like the rich and famous. Staying at Marsten's would be an adjustment. He wasn't sure how professional it was, but he decided she deserved to have some forewarning. "Actually, yes, your uncle is worth several billion dollars. Again, I assumed you knew."

She gave him the strangest look. He wasn't sure she believed him.

"I... you're not kidding?"

"No, not at all."

She sighed, leaned against the back door, and closed her eyes. "I should have known," she whispered even softer than before. Maybe she was talking to herself. She opened her eyes and met his again. "It does make sense. Now that I think about it. So many...well, it's fine. I guess I should be glad. I was worried about being in the way at his ranch, but if the place is that big, maybe I won't feel like such an inconvenience."

Why did he feel like he just gave her bad news? Most people would be thrilled to find out their uncle was a multi-billionaire. Brynnan looked like her dog died. He couldn't stand seeing the sadness in her eyes all over again. And this time he wasn't even sure why it was there.

"Sorry about the confusion," he said. *What more can I say? Why is this job so full of awkward conversations?* He looked at his watch. "Is there anything else we can get loaded for you? If you're ready, I think your uncle would like to leave soon."

"No. No, I'll just grab my purse."

She stepped passed him, looking more weary than she did when he walked in. Which was saying something.

It was decided Brynnan and Jack would take her 4Runner, and Cody would drive Marsten back in his car. Marsten seemed to want some privacy to make several phone calls on the trip back, plus, Jack could tell Marsten wasn't comfortable with the idea of Brynnan driving to the ranch alone. In fact, he seemed overly protective of her. Good to know. That didn't bother Jack a bit. Because he had a gut feeling Brynnan might need protection.

Jack followed Brynnan to the garage while she fished around in her purse for the keys. Neither of them walked to the passenger side of the car.

"I don't mind driving," he said.

"Oh, it's okay, I can—" she stopped mid-sentence and gave him a curious look. For the first time since he'd met her, she reminded him of her uncle. Her eyes looked right through him. Analyzing. Assessing.

He shifted his weight under a surreal sense she was trying to read his mind. And possibly succeeding. "You've had a tough few days. I don't mind driving," he offered again.

He was still under her microscope.

Finally, she...grinned?

"You want to drive, don't you?" she asked.

Yep. She was grinning. But he had no idea why.

"Sure. If that's okay. What's so funny?"

"I think you really *want* to drive. I think you're one of those guys. I don't think it would matter what kind of week I've had. You just don't like riding shotgun."

Wow. If she could tell that by staring him down, he was in trouble. Maybe more trouble than he wanted to consider at the moment.

"I didn't know I was so obvious. Look, no offense, I just, like you said, I like to drive." Actually, he loved to drive. And he *hated* riding shotgun, or worse, the backseat. If he was in a car, he wanted to be behind the wheel. His stomach flipped. She might find that offensive. She might think he thought she still didn't have it together enough to drive or, *so much worse*, she might assume he had something against women driving.

But then that grin turned into the most beautiful smile he'd ever seen.

"It's fine," she laughed. "I'm not offended. I

51

can tell you really want to be in the driver's seat. So, for the record, I'm doing you a favor," she tossed him the keys, "and not the other way around."

"Understood."

She walked around to the passenger's side and he couldn't stifle his smile. Wow, this girl was something else. He realized he was not dreading spending two and a half hours in the car with her. Not one bit.

They talked most of the way to the ranch.

He asked about her career, and where she went to college.

He couldn't believe they both graduated from Texas A&M.

"So, you're coming *back* to College Station. The Brazos Valley isn't new to you."

"No, not at all. I grew up in Austin, but I was in College Station for six years. For my undergrad, then a masters."

He'd graduated from the Corps of Cadets at A&M three years before she graduated with a degree in history. She added she also had a master's in history from the University of Texas and had since then, briefly worked in the history departments of two other universities out of state. Her gratefulness for the new position at A&M was evident in her voice.

"You wanted to move back to Texas, I guess? To be closer to your parents?" *Oh man, should he have said that?*

An uncomfortable expression crossed her face. "Oh, I guess partly. I definitely love being back in Texas."

He decided to shift the conversation. He was born and raised an Aggie, so it was easy to joke about the rival universities.

"I know, I know. Both my parents went to UT, so they were pleased that I finally went there for a degree. And I honestly had a fantastic experience there but," she lowered her voice to a whisper, "I promise I'm really an Aggie." She laughed for the second time that day. He could get used to hearing her laugh.

He noticed Cody slow in front of him. They were coming up on a road closure. Strange. He didn't see any construction. They followed the detour sign directing them off the highway and down a road that was little more than two ruts through a field.

Something was wrong. TXDot wouldn't detour highway traffic through a pasture.

They were about to crest a small hill. He didn't have a line of sight past the top of the rise. The hairs on the back of Jack's neck stood rigid.

He hit the brakes and called Marsten.

"Yes?"

"We need to turn around, sir."

"The sign—"

"Yes, sir, I know, but I don't have a good feeling about this. Let's get back to the highway. We can turn around and find another route."

There was a pause. "Okay, we'll turn around."

Jack turned around and was back at the highway in about ten seconds. And he paled.

Brynnan straightened. She looked the way he felt.

"Where are the road closure sign and detour signs? They were there just a minute ago," she said.

Jack hit the gas and prayed Cody would stay close behind. "We're getting out of here."

He sped down the highway, in the opposite direction. Cody stayed on his bumper. Good man.

He looked at Brynnan. "Can you pull up GPS on your phone? Find us a different route? I don't care about the distance so much. I just don't want to take an obvious route to the ranch."

She stared at him. And didn't move. Maybe he shouldn't have asked—

"Yes, I've got it." She pulled out her phone. "But I have a few questions for you in a minute. And I want answers." She stated it like a threat.

Nice. Anything he said would likely upset her. And saying anything at all would probably upset his boss. Marsten had all but spelled out that he didn't want to discuss possible threats in front of Brynnan. He meant well but, keeping Brynnan in the dark wasn't going to be possible.

She routed him to a nearby farm-to-market road that would hit a different highway after ten miles. That would work. He called Marsten and relayed the new route.

"I saw the signs were removed," said Marsten.

"Yes, sir. It's beyond suspicious, but it's not enough to involve the police."

"I understand. Is Brynnan okay?"

Jack chanced a glance in her direction. Not happy. "Yes, sir, she's fine. However, with your permission, she'd like an explanation."

Her eyes showed she approved of that comment.

But this time Marsten's pause was so long Jack was afraid the call had dropped. "Sir?"

Marsten cleared his throat. "Explain anything you think is necessary. She's smart. I believe I forgot to mention that. She'll figure out all our concerns anyway. I was just trying to delay her having to process one more thing."

"I understand, sir."

"Thank you, Jack. Hopefully the rest of the trip will be uneventful."

"Yes, sir." Jack ended the call.

'Uneventful' for Marsten maybe, but he was afraid his ride with Brynnan was about to turn uncomfortable.

He glanced at her. Her gaze bore into him.

He tried organizing what he should say.

"Jack?"

"Yes?"

"You're stalling. You don't look like you know how to tell me whatever it is you don't want to tell me. Let me help you out. How about I ask you some questions and you try to answer as best you can?"

She sounded like she was talking to an eight-year-old. But when he looked at her, her eyes weren't condescending. He saw a mix of understanding and fear. She wasn't naïve. And she wanted to know the truth.

"Ok, shoot."

"Do you think someone deliberately put those detour signs out to get us, and only us, off the main road, then after we were headed where they wanted, they removed the signs?"

"I think it's very possible," he said, his tone perfectly even.

Brynnan nodded. "Why are you here?"

"Excuse me?"

"Why did you come to Austin with Marsten? Is he worried about someone attacking him? Is that what you think was about to happen back there on that dirt road? Do you think that's why that guy broke in and shot at us the other night? Is someone after Marsten?"

Jack took his eyes off the road long enough to read exasperated confusion on her face. And the fear in her eyes. Not a clueless, panicking fear. A knowing fear.

He needed to level with her.

He drew his eyes back to the road and blew out a long breath.

"First of all, you need to know we have no solid proof that Marsten or you are in any danger. I initially came to Austin because your uncle received some threats by email and we hadn't had a chance to investigate them, so I came along, just in case. Just after we got to your parents' house that first night, I found out those were empty threats. I'm sure they have nothing to do with the intruder or the detour signs."

"So, what *is* going on? You think you know why that guy broke in the other night? And you think that detour trap back there is related?"

"I don't know who he is. I'm saying it's all very suspicious. Your uncle pays me to be suspicious, to err on the side of caution. So, that's what we're doing."

Maybe that's enough of an answer for her.

"What aren't you telling me?"

Nope. She wanted more answers. Great.

And her tone was intense. He looked her way

long enough to wonder if she was about to hit him or start crying. He'd rather she hit him.

Lord, help me be honest without scaring her.

"I'm not trying to be dishonest with you. Your uncle doesn't want me to worry you when we don't have proof of anything. You've obviously had a very rough few days. He doesn't want to cause you needless stress."

She sighed and shook her head. "Marsten is very sweet. I love my uncle, I do, but something he hasn't learned about me is that one of my biggest fears is of the unknown. Having all the facts about something is what helps me deal with things. Telling me you're suspicious and not telling me all the reasons you're suspicious, is *terrifying*. You have no idea where my mind is running right now. So *please*, tell me everything you're thinking."

Marsten underestimated Brynnan. That, Jack was sure of. Maybe his boss could look into those wide, brown eyes and dance around the truth, but Jack didn't have it in him. If Marsten didn't like it, he'd deal with the fallout later.

"Ok. The intruder from the other night didn't strike me as a common thief. He picked the lock on the back door. And I'd just made a security lap less than two minutes before. Which means he was able to do it quickly. As a side note," he looked at Brynnan, "that door should've had a dead bolt. I don't know why it didn't. But you need to make sure your new condo has a lock and a dead bolt on all exterior doors, okay?"

"Yes, don't worry. It will."

Jack gave a nod and continued. "The guy didn't tell the police anything, but he lawyered up so fast his lawyer was actually at the hospital before the police left. Again, not normal."

He could tell she was nodding in his peripheral vision. Then he felt her eyes on him.

"What's wrong?"

"What else aren't you telling me?"

He gripped the steering wheel tighter. Everything else was more personal. More disturbing.

The tension in the car was palpable. He turned the AC up a notch. It didn't help.

"Ms. Marsh," he kept his voice low and gentle, "please remember it's my job to be suspicious, paranoid even, okay? I can't ignore coincidences. I have to be thorough. To listen to my instincts."

"I understand. Just tell me." She sounded calmer now. But no way was she going to back down.

He took a deep breath and prayed he was doing the right thing. "Your parents' accident was caused by a black Audi. There was a witness across the street at a gas station. The Audi forced them off the road and they hit a tree. Then, the Audi pulled over, the driver got out, walked to their car, opened the passenger's side door for a moment, closed it and took off again. It's odd. Usually people who flee a hit-and-run don't get out of their car. It's possible he saw the extent of your parents' injuries and *then* panicked, but I'm not confident of that. The police haven't found him yet. I can't ignore that an *armed* intruder picked his way into your parents' home just hours later. And...your uncle told me your grandfather is Bobby Alesi. Then the very suspect detour sign... All together it's too much to ignore."

Heavy silence hung between them. He glanced her way a couple of times, but she'd turned to her window.

After several painfully silent seconds, she whispered, "Thank you for telling me," just barely loud enough for him to hear.

The quiet resumed. She was understandably upset. And it was killing him.

Before he knew what he was doing, he slipped his hand into hers and squeezed. "Brynnan,"

She didn't turn. But she held onto his hand.

"Brynnan, please look at me."

After a moment of hesitation, her eyes met his. He squeezed her hand again. "It's going to be okay. We're almost back to the ranch. I have a team on the way. We'll get it all figured out. You're safe. Trust me, okay?"

Her eyes held at least a flicker of trust. He hoped he wasn't imagining that. She squeezed his hand gently and let go. And he pretended her touch didn't send electricity through his arm. *Stay focused. She's your boss's niece.*

She was still looking at him, but he couldn't read her expression.

"So, what's your background? Law enforcement or military? You sound like you've handled things like this before." Her voice sounded wary. Like she was nervous about the answer.

"Military."

She turned to him looking...*relieved?* Why? Oh. She had experience with the FBI. Maybe she didn't want to think about that.

"What branch?"

"Army."

The penetrating look she used to analyze him with before tossing him the car keys returned. He felt her gaze raking over him.

"Special Ops?"

How did she...? "Yes," he answered.

"Rangers?"

"Yes. Why did you guess Special Ops?"

"Partly a guess."

"And what was the other part?"

She narrowed her eyes at him, but there was no condemnation. He wasn't exactly sure what was spinning through her head. Which was unsettling. Because apparently, she could read *him* easily.

"The way you handled the shooter the other night. Not just that you shot him—it was the *way* you acted that night. And your wariness about...everything else you mentioned. Your last job obviously wasn't behind a desk. And you like being in charge."

"Is that bad?"

"For some people. But you're not the domineering type. There's a difference." When he didn't immediately respond she added, "That's a compliment."

"Thanks."

"Special Ops is impressive. Thank you for your service."

"Thank you."

She might have smiled, but he was trying to keep his eyes on the road. Her comments knocked him off balance. He found that perplexing, unnerving and very attractive. Oh, no.

Change. The. Subject.

"What did my uncle tell you about Alesi? I mean...about things that happened in the past?"

To anything but that.

Why couldn't they just talk about the weather

or something? *Anything* but her tortured past or present dangers. Her voice alone exposed what she was thinking—what she hoped he didn't know.

But he wasn't going to lie to her.

"He told me you were kidnapped when you were sixteen. And eighteen."

At that, she whipped her head back to her window, and Jack wondered if he would see anything but the back of her head before they got to the ranch. Maybe he should just keep his mouth shut and drive. But he sensed she was hurting. He had to say something.

"Brynnan, you may wish he hadn't told me anything, or feel like he betrayed your privacy. But please look at it another way. I'm glad he told me— only because knowing that information can help me keep you safe. It allows me to see the bigger picture and be better prepared for possible threats, in case any of this is connected."

He heard a quiet "Thank you."

And they pulled up to the entrance to Kade Ranch.

Both cars parked near the front door of the main house. Marsten explained which room Brynnan would be staying in and Jack headed inside with two of her bags. When he returned to the foyer, Felix Hanes was standing near the door rubbing his hands on his jeans, looking as awkward as ever.

"Is she here?"

Jack's jaw clenched. Felix sounded way too eager. "Yes, she's here."

"Can I meet her?"

Jack tried to remain professional. Felix could

61

be annoying. Social interactions were not his forte.

Jack understood why Marsten hired the shaggy-blonde twenty-something though—his techy skills were off the chart. He could do anything he wanted to with a computer. Talent aside, however, Jack decided he needed to keep a close eye on the tech's methods—he couldn't shake his initial suspicion that the young tech had used his skills beyond the parameters of the law in the past.

"You'll meet her...just..." How did he say this? "play it cool, Mr. Hanes."

Felix looked through the front window. "She's pretty!" He said, too loudly, too excitedly and too much like a desperate groupie who had never talked to a girl before.

"Mr. Hanes," Jack said, with a glare that made Felix recoil.

"What? I just—"

Jack shot him another look, efficiently silencing him.

Felix wasn't wrong of course. But that was irrelevant.

The front door opened and Marsten led Brynnan into the foyer, instructing Cody to take the rest of her bags to her room. Annalee materialized out of nowhere, enveloped Brynnan in a hug and asked, no less than three times, if she needed anything. Apparently, the mother hen of the property had met Brynnan before. *But I thought Brynnan had never been to any of Marsten's houses?*

Marsten looked relieved Annalee was mothering Brynnan so much. He probably figured Brynnan could benefit from Annalee's unique skill set right now.

Felix cleared his throat less than eloquently.

Marsten gestured the young tech forward. "Ah, yes. Brynnan, this is Felix Hanes, a very gifted IT specialist I was fortunate to hire."

Felix beamed at the compliment and thrust out his hand. "Nice to meet you," he said, shaking her hand a little too long.

Jack fought the urge to roll his eyes, and subtly guided the drooling IT specialist away.

"Jack," said Marsten, "as soon as Brynnan gets settled, could you issue her a key card, and any security codes she may need? I want her to feel free to access any part of the property."

"Of course, sir." He turned to Brynnan. "I'll stop by your room in a few minutes."

"Thank you," she said with a smile he was very relieved to see. The trip here had been...intense. But she didn't seem to be holding anything against him. He hoped.

"Brynnan there are a few others I would like you to meet." Marsten gave Jack a nod and led his niece toward the kitchen.

Jack noticed Felix gawking after them and wanted to kick him. But he restrained himself. For now. "Mr. Hanes, go back to work."

Felix shrugged and shuffled off.

Jack knew it wasn't really his place to give Felix orders, but he acted like such a child it was difficult not to keep him in check.

Jack shoved Felix from his mind and returned to his office. He coded a key card for Brynnan and printed out the punch code for the front gate, the pool area, the greenhouse, and a few doors she might want access to during her stay. Ten minutes later he knocked on the door of her guest suite.

"Oh, hi. Please, come in." She stepped back from the door to let him enter.

The room was large, a suite similar to his, but without a kitchenette in the corner. An antique bed full of pillows and white duvet sat on one end, and on the opposite end of the room, facing a small sofa, stood a woodburning fireplace outlined in vintage tiles, complete with a large, intricately carved mantle.

When he turned to face her, he knew he wanted to say something more than 'Here's your key.'

"Did Cody unload everything you need?"

"Yes, thanks."

"He'll keep your car in the garage," he reached into his pocket, "and here are your keys. Thanks, by the way, for letting me drive."

"No problem." She rewarded him with a genuine smile that relaxed him and quickened his pulse at the same time. Man, her smile had more effect on him than he was comfortable with. Not good.

He cleared his throat and handed her the key card he coded. "This is your key. And here is a list of access codes for the front gate, garage, etc.," he said, handing her the piece of paper. "You may not need them, but your uncle wants you to feel at home and have access to anything you need."

"Thank you," she repeated. "Everyone is being so kind. I don't want to be an inconvenience."

Jack smiled. "You are not at all an inconvenience."

He'd seen sparks of confidence and intelligence in her eyes when he was in Austin and was relieved to see those traits stronger in her now. It baffled him how she appeared so resilient yet vulnerable all at the same time. And he was certain everything he was thinking about her in that moment was anything but professional.

He cleared his throat again. "If there's anything else you need, my cell number is at the bottom of the paper, under the access codes."

"Thanks." She really needed to say more. So much more. Now that she'd processed everything Jack had said in the car, she had so many questions.

But she had trust issues. Serious trust issues. She didn't talk to people about her fears—about the very real and present dangers she knew all too well. Her parents consistently diverted the conversation when she mentioned her concerns. And Marsten, well, Marsten had always seemed more worried about her than her parents were. She never understood that. But even he didn't discuss anything with her. She was convinced now that he simply didn't want to say anything that might upset her.

So, she learned to keep her worries to herself. All these years. So, how was she supposed to talk to this man standing in front of her? But she wanted to. Or maybe needed to.

"Jack, what you said in the car...what do you really think is going on? I'm not ready to consider that my parents' accident was anything but an accident, but...the rest of it...I agree, it can't all be a coincidence, can it?"

She couldn't believe how much empathy she saw in his eyes. Somehow, he understood her fear.

"I don't know anything more than I told you. Yet. But I promise, I'm looking into everything as much as I can. And I'm increasing the security around here. You're safe here. So, try to rest and relax. Enjoy Annalee's cooking. Explore the house. There's a library and a gym."

She raised her eyebrows. "Of course, there is."

"What's wrong?"

How could she explain? "Oh, it's just...everything here is wonderful, really, it is but, all I can think about is *why didn't I know?*" She sighed. "I don't like my family keeping secrets from me. About anything. My parents and Marsten, I've learned over the years, have kept all kinds of things from me. This is just one more."

Ah. That explains her initial reaction back in Austin.

"Well, on the bright side, this isn't such a terrible family secret as family secrets go. You can at least take advantage of the pool while you're here, and I'm going to repeat, enjoy Annalee's cooking."

"Oh, I know I will. I've enjoyed her cooking many times. I just love Annalee, she's always been so wonderful to me."

It was none of his business, but he had to ask. "So, how is it you know Annalee? Since you haven't been to any of your uncle's homes?"

"Oh, right. I guess that sounds strange. Well, as far back as I can remember Marsten would bring Annalee to meet us for holidays. Annalee would do all the cooking. I knew she worked for him, cooked for him, so yeah, I knew he wasn't destitute, but I had no idea he had a *staff*. I just knew he desperately needed Annalee because he was hopeless in the kitchen."

"I'm getting that impression. I learned

recently he can't make coffee," Jack said with a grin.

"I'm not surprised. Marsten has never been able to make toast, much less a meal—believe me, I watched him try once." She smiled at the memory. "And, there were times, when my parents were overseas and I was sick or something, he would bring Annalee with him to check on me. She was always so genuine and kind. I realize it's her job, but I think she really enjoys caring for people."

"I think she does too. I can tell she's very glad you're here. I am too." *Oh no, did I just say that? Did it sound simply polite? Or inappropriate? Change the subject.*

"But back to your earlier request, I promise I won't keep you in the dark. If I learn anything that relates to your safety, I'll let you know."

"Or Marsten's."

"Well, you ask your uncle about that. If he's fine with it, I'll tell you anything you want to know. But I will say, at the moment, I don't know anything about specific threats to your uncle outside of everything we've discussed."

"Thank you."

His reassurances relieved her. She should feel calm now. But instead, she remembered him squeezing her hand, and she realized she wished he would do that again. Her heart skipped a beat. Oh, no. She needed to get him out of her room before she embarrassed herself.

"Thanks for the keys. Sorry if I kept you too long."

"No problem at all. I'll see you later."

He left, and she realized how exhausted she was. She was curious, but a little apprehensive about exploring the historic Kade mansion. It could wait.

Right now, the king-size, four poster bed was calling to her. She collapsed on the bed and fell asleep wondering what else she didn't know about her uncle.

❧

The next afternoon Jack was building a sandwich for his lunch when Annalee practically pounced on him.

"So, what do you think of Miss Marsh? She's pretty, isn't she? Such a sweet girl, don't you think?"

"Yes, Ma'am. She's very nice," said Jack as neutrally as possible, in an attempt to derail Annalee from the track she was barreling down.

"Yes, poor thing. Bless her heart. What she's going through must be so awful. I'm so glad Mr. Kade talked her into coming here. She needs to be surrounded by encouraging people right now. She's been in my prayers ever since I heard about what happened to her mama and daddy. Oh, the poor thing." She looked at Jack as if he was supposed to say something.

Before he had time to respond, a timer went off and Annalee rushed to the oven to retrieve something. "I'm just sick about what happened, of course, but I'm so glad she's visiting here for a while. She's such a sweet thing."

"I didn't realize until yesterday that you two knew each other."

"Oh, yes, I've watched her grow up. Mr. Kade would meet her and her parents somewhere for Christmas every year. And Thanksgiving. They'd go to a big cabin in Colorado or somewhere. I always went with him, to do all the cooking. And there were other times...if Brynnan ever needed anything... Her parents were out of the country often, so if she wasn't feeling well, or Mr. Kade just wanted to check on her, he would take me with him." She winked at him and quieted her voice. "He would say he needed me to go because Brynnan liked my cooking, and so they wouldn't have to eat out every meal. But really, especially when she was sick, I think he wanted me to go with him to mother over her. He wanted to help, but, bless his heart, he had no clue how to take care of young girl with the flu. And he definitely couldn't help her figure out how to take a shower when she broke her leg."

"Her parents really weren't around much?" He watched Brynnan grieve her parents' deaths. There was no doubt she loved them. But there was also a sense they didn't share a strong bond. Not like he had with his family. Even through all his deployments, Jack enjoyed a close relationship with his parents and two brothers. He didn't get the same impression about Brynnan and her parents, though he wasn't sure why.

Annalee's natural smile pressed into a thin line. "No. They were very busy. Always working at some archeological dig site, or researching, or whatnot." She didn't meet his eyes, wringing her hands on her apron.

"I see. But all that time, they never visited Marsten?"

"No, they never came to Houston. To Mr. Kade's house, I mean. Or to any of his properties."

"Why?"

"Well," she lowered her voice again,

smoothed out her apron, and glanced toward the door to make sure they were indeed alone. "Mr. Kade was good to his brother. He really was. They actually seemed surprisingly close considering Jonathan was ten years younger. But I think Mr. Kade was afraid Jonathan wouldn't feel comfortable at one of his estates. You see, Jonathan wasn't a Kade, he was only Mr. Kade's half-brother. After Roger Kade, Marsten's father, passed away, Marsten's mother remarried, and she and her second husband had Jonathan. All this," she gestured to the grand home they were standing in, "is all Kade money. Jonathan wasn't raised like this, and so neither was Brynnan."

"But didn't Roger Kade's wife inherit his estate?"

"Well, obviously that was a long time ago, and it's really not my business, but what I heard is that she didn't want it. Not much anyway. She didn't want to put up with the Kade family affairs, politics and expectations. She loved Roger Kade, but the Kade family...not so much. She gave Roger's inheritance to Marsten. The Kade family groomed Marsten through his teen years to be, well, a Kade. Jonathan didn't have those kinds of expectations forced on him. He and Marsten were close though. Of course, that's just what I hear. I've only worked for Mr. Kade for about twenty-five years. All that happened before my time."

She shook her head slowly. "Bless her heart. Brynnan, I mean. She probably feels very out of place here. I know she's not used to all this. Oh, bless her sweet heart."

Annalee's broad smile returned as she finally swung back around to the reason she'd started the whole exchange. "She really is a pretty girl, isn't she?"

"Yes, Ma'am." He tried to sound no more than polite in his answer. What he thought of Brynnan Marsh was really none of Annalee Ames' business, but he was pretty sure she didn't see it that way. "Ms. Ames," he continued before she had a chance to suggest anything else, "thank you for the sandwich. If you don't mind, I'm going to take it back to my office. I have a lot of work to do."

"Oh, of course, of course. Go ahead. You need something to drink too. I'm making some fresh tea. You go on. I'll bring it over to you."

"You don't have to do that ma'am."

"Oh, it's no trouble. You can't eat that mountain of a sandwich you made without something to wash it down. I'll bring you some tea. Is sweet okay?" Annalee always assumed people wanted her sugary default beverage.

"Yes, ma'am, that would be fine. Thank you."

"And I almost forgot, Mr. Kade requested dinner served at six thirty tonight. On the terrace, if it's not too hot. Otherwise, I'll serve in the dining room. Did he mention that to you already?"

"Yes, he did. Six thirty. I'll be there. Thank you, Ms. Ames."

Jack had been told Marsten Kade often invited his staff to dinner, one at a time, in an effort to strengthen relationships with his employees. So, he wasn't surprised at the invitation to dinner, but he wished he had some sort of significant update to share. He learned absolutely nothing useful in the past twenty-four hours about anything that had happened in Austin, or regarding their detour on the highway. Maybe they could just focus on security improvements to the ranch. Those were issues he could easily address.

~

At six twenty-eight, Jack reached for the door leading out to the terrace when he heard a voice behind him.

"Hello. Marsten said you'd be joining us for dinner. I'm glad."

Jack was surprised to see Brynnan, but maybe he shouldn't have been. It made sense she would join her uncle for dinner.

They exchanged the usual polite pleasantries.

He held the door for her, followed her onto the terrace, and immediately appreciated the view. He'd studied every inch of the Kade property from a security standpoint, but he'd never spent time on the extensive terrace taking in the sprawling landscape of manicured gardens and gently rolling hills dotted with massive oak trees. It was a scene worthy of formal parties with a live orchestra serenading dancing couples into the wee hours of the morning. Personally, Jack would love to enjoy the view with his feet propped up in a lounge chair next to a fire pit.

Neither scene would play out tonight.

But he couldn't complain about the company. Marsten was in a very amiable mood, and Brynnan was smiling more and more. He was relieved to see her more relaxed, almost happy.

The evening was less muggy than an average June evening in Central Texas. A thunderstorm was forecast for later that evening and the foretelling clouds had already arrived. The overcast sky and a welcomed breeze brought the temperature down to the upper seventies.

Annalee served chicken spaghetti, green beans, a fresh fruit salad and peppered cornbread muffins. The conversation circled around the impending weather, Annalee's excellent cooking, a thankfulness for a lack of mosquitoes, and eventually, improvements for security at the ranch and Marsten's other properties. Less pleasant topics were avoided by unspoken, mutual consent.

Brynnan enjoyed the evening, becoming better acquainted with both Jack and her uncle. She found one more fascinating than the other, but she kept her attention evenly allotted.

She was beginning to comprehend the vast nature of her uncle's wealth, which was definitely interesting, but she felt more impressed with Jack's military service. There was so much about both of them she suddenly wanted to know.

She was glad Jack was asking her uncle so many questions. He had a professional excuse to inquire about the ranch, Marsten's other properties, and how often he visited them, whereas coming from her, the questions might have sounded intrusive.

Jack shifted his focus to Brynnan. "I apologize. I didn't mean to monopolize the conversation."

"Don't apologize, it's actually very interesting." She gave her uncle a teasing look of reprimand. "Apparently there are a lot of things about Marsten I didn't know."

Marsten shrugged with a feigned look of

innocence. "Ah, well, I never thought my properties would be an interesting subject of conversation to you."

He made it sound so simple. No big deal. And she knew he meant no harm in keeping her in the dark all those years. She still wished she'd known, not that it would've changed anything—she just felt embarrassed being so clueless. But, then again, what was he supposed to say, 'hey, by the way, I'm rich?'

Marsten pushed his chair back and laid his napkin on the table. "I hate to leave, but I have several things to attend to this evening. Please, stay out here as long as you like. Enjoy the cool air before the rain gets here."

Jack stood and shook Marsten's hand. "Thank you, sir."

"Goodnight, Jack. And goodnight, Brynnan. I'll ask Annalee to check in on you."

Marsten disappeared into the house, and instantly, Annalee appeared on the terrace offering coffee, Homemade Vanilla Blue Bell ice cream and peach cobbler, with a very pleased—and way too obvious—look on her face.

Jack wondered if Brynnan felt like their evening just evolved into an ambush date as much as he did. Marsten didn't seem the type to arrange such a thing. But, anticipating the opportunity to throw unknowing couples together, in hopes of sparking chemistry, seemed etched into Annalee's DNA.

The gleam in her eye, when she insisted the two ambush victims take their dessert with them on a walk through the gardens, left no doubt as to her intentions.

Jack decided the safest plan of action was to take his cue from Brynnan. To his relief, she broke into a gracious smile, accepted a bowl of ice cream, and thanked Annalee for the suggestion about the gardens, as if nothing awkward was happening.

Since Brynnan obliged, and because Jack realized following Annalee's recommendation was the quickest way to get rid of her, he gladly relieved Annalee of his bowl of ice cream and the pair headed toward the gardens, far from prying eyes from kitchen windows.

How was he supposed to navigate this? He wasn't quite sure what Brynnan was thinking, though she was likely simply being polite. He was absolutely *certain* about what Annalee was thinking, but she was just going to have to get over it. Entertaining the idea of anything romantic with his boss's niece would be clearly unprofessional. And even if it wasn't, he wasn't going to subject himself to that kind of rejection again.

He should have known better. Should have learned his lesson from his experience with Heather. But sucker that he was, he put his heart out there again a few months later. When he met Megan.

Things started out well. Then one night they stopped for gas on the way to a friend's house to watch a football game. They both entered the convenience store to pick up some drinks, and while they were inside, two armed men stormed in, waving guns, demanding money, and yelling for everyone to freeze. Megan panicked. She tried to run out the door before Jack could stop her. One of the gunmen aimed his weapon directly at her. Jack tackled him as he fired, his shot hitting the ceiling. He wrestled the gun away and quickly rendered the shooter unconscious. He was forced to shoot the guy's accomplice a moment later when he came at him with his gun.

He'd acted on instinct. His military training served him well that night. He saved Megan's life. The police commended his actions, even called him a hero. But Megan didn't run into his arms. Not that night or ever again.

She agreed his actions were warranted, but she realized she didn't want to be with someone capable of taking a life. She hadn't seen him as a protector, she just saw the violence.

He was shocked. He served in Special Forces. She knew that. What did she think he did when he was deployed?

He reasoned later, as time went on, that it was a good thing Megan left when she did. It would have been harder had she left while he was deployed again, or after the relationship turned serious. Things hadn't progressed that far. He'd been thankful for that, at least.

After two failed relationship attempts, he resigned himself to the fact that no woman worth pursuing was going to accept, much less love, the seasoned soldier he'd become.

Which was why the memory of Brynnan in his arms a few nights ago in Austin threw him off balance. He shot the intruder. She'd been frightened. But she let him comfort her. He felt her relax into his chest. She even thanked him.

He wasn't sure how to process that. Or maybe he was afraid to.

The nearing storm darkened the sky and dropped the temperature a few more degrees. The unseasonably cool air felt wonderful as they meandered through the gardens enjoying the brilliant azaleas, knock-out roses, and hibiscus as best they could in the low light.

Brynnan was more at peace than she had been since she arrived. "I need to come out here tomorrow, in the daylight. I didn't realize the gardens were this elaborate. And it's all so beautiful." She inhaled the night air deeply and felt even more relaxed. "I can't imagine what kind of impression I gave you in Austin. I feel like I'm just now stepping out of a haze. Everything since...since the accident, has just been a blur."

"You didn't give a bad impression at all. You've been through a lot. And I think you're doing great."

She gave a shy smile. "Thanks. God had to pick me up and carry me through this week. I know my parents are with Him, and I know everything will be fine, it was all just such a shock."

She spoke about her faith with comfortable confidence. He'd heard her make similar remarks back in Austin, and he was relieved her faith was strong. It made him worry about her a little less. Unfortunately for him, it did nothing to make him less attracted to her.

Wait. Was he really attracted to her? Noticing that a woman was attractive and admiring some of her qualities didn't mean he was necessarily attracted *to* her. He just needed to stop thinking about her that way. Which was going to be so easy right now, walking alone through the beautiful gardens together like they were on a date or something.

The breeze picked up and she tried to wrangle flying strands of her soft, brown hair behind her ears.

She asked where he lived and he explained he was living in the main house, for the time being. "Your uncle wanted me to start right away, so I'm living on the property for now. It makes things easier, in a way, but eventually I'll look for my own place."

She watched him rake his hand through his hair. Why was she wondering what his own place might be like?

She wanted to ask more about him. All she knew about him was college and the military. And that his chin cleared the top of her head by a good two inches.

"How do you like living back in Texas? You're practically living in your hometown again."

"Yeah, there are lots of things I like about being back. But between Annalee's cooking and occasionally eating at my parents' house, I'm going to have to keep up with the exercise regime I had in the military."

"I'm guessing this job isn't as exciting as Special Ops, but Marsten seems to really like you. Take that as a huge compliment. I think he's usually 'all or nothing' about people. He either really trusts and admires them or is barely civil with them."

"Really? Well, honestly, that tracks with the impression I have of him so far."

His easy smile warmed her. Maybe too much. This probably wasn't a good idea. She didn't need to get *too* friendly with her uncle's head of security. But Jack was somehow very easy to talk to. She felt inexplicably comfortable around him. *But why?* She barely knew him. And she didn't usually trust the people she *did* know. Life was easier that way. Safer.

They turned a corner and her sleeve caught on a thorny rose bush.

Fantastic.

She reached around and tried to untangle herself from the branch, but her one-handed effort wasn't very efficient.

"Here, I got it," he said.

Working to extricate her sleeve from the thorns, his arm brushed hers.

She hadn't stood this close to him since that first night in Austin, when he embraced her. His subtle masculine scent filled her senses. He wasn't a cologne kind of guy, but whether it was aftershave or fabric softener, the woodsy scent calmed her. She wondered if she'd ever bury her head in his chest again. *Ugh. Why were her thoughts going there?* She needed to stop looking at his sculpted arms and broad shoulders... *No. Stop staring. Stop staring.*

Maybe he didn't notice.

She met his eyes. *Yep, he noticed.*

He'd freed her shirt of the rose bush. Her face flushed.

She started shoving her hair behind her ears because, well, she had to do *something,* and her voice was caught in her throat.

Embarrassing.

Before the moment became ridiculously uncomfortable, the sky mercifully ripped open, unleashing a proper Texas downpour. They took off, racing for the closest entrance to the main house, though the running was probably pointless—after a few seconds they were soaked to the bone.

Finding an unlocked door leading to the library off the foyer, they finally stepped out of the deluge. Neither of them had a dry thread on their bodies.

Jack worked to shut the door against the wind. His drenched shirt stuck to his skin, leaving nothing to her imagination as to his fitness level. *Do. Not. Stare.*

Thankfully, as he shut the door, his attention was focused on something outside the window and not on the pathetic drowned rat ogling at his chiseled physique.

"That wind is giving the south gate a hard time. Buck is probably aware, but I'll mention it to him."

Brynnan nodded, and noticed all the water they'd brought in. "Oh, no. We should—"

A mixture of squeaky giggles and mischievous laughter at the library door cut her off. Mora and Julie made no attempt to contain their amusement at the scene. Nor did they attempt to avert their stares. At Jack.

"Don't worry, don't worry. We'll take care of all the water," said Julie, her eyes all over Jack. "You probably want to get out of those clothes and into a hot shower..." Okay, now Julie was just outright flirting.

And that shouldn't bother her. But it did. But it shouldn't.

I think I'm getting a headache.

Jack quickly apologized for the mess without directly responding to Julie, and guided Brynnan to the foyer. He offered to return the half-eaten, and now watered-down bowls of ice cream to Annalee.

Brynnan could still hear Julie and Mora giggling in the library and now, felt Annalee's eyes on them around an almost-closed kitchen door. She was hesitant to leave Jack's company, but she was grateful to escape the awkwardness. She thanked him and sloshed off to her room.

Jack entered the kitchen to find Annalee pretending to clean something on the floor near the door.

"You're too obvious, Ms. Ames," Jack said.

"Oh, for heaven's sake Jack, you're going to have to start calling me Annalee." She grinned at him like a Cheshire cat. "Sooo?"

"So, what?" He gave her a teasing glare. "Now Annalee, you need to slow down on this...this plotting of yours."

"I'm not plotting. You two hit it off at the very beginning, on your own. I could see that. So, all I'm doing is nudging a bit."

"I see. Well, don't 'nudge' just yet. She buried her parents a few days ago. She has a lot going on. And I've only worked here for a week. Besides the fact that Mr. Kade probably wouldn't appreciate me pursuing a less than professional relationship with his grieving niece."

"Whatever you say, whatever you say, of course," she said, floating away with the ice cream bowls, still grinning.

Brynnan couldn't sleep. She tossed and turned, re-fluffed her pillow and checked her phone.

Two a.m. Nighttime was the worst—when she was alone with her thoughts and sleep eluded her. She knew she was still grieving, but she wasn't sure what stage of grief she was in. Weren't they supposed to happen in some kind of order? Hadn't she heard that somewhere? That's not what this felt like though. She drifted back and forth between denial and acceptance, then back to denial, then back to acceptance, with moments of anger and depression thrown in here and there. Regret surfaced. And questions.

She hoped to reconnect with her parents this summer. She didn't even get to say goodbye.

Marsten was her only relative now. The only person she considered family anyway. There was her mother's side, of course, but she didn't think of them as family. She'd been afraid some of them might attend the funeral. She wasn't sure she could handle that. She still didn't know if any of them had. She wouldn't recognize many of them. Several strangers attended the service. She briefly wondered who they were. They never spoke to her. Could they have been from the Alesi side?

She rolled onto her side and pushed the strangers from her mind. Wondering about them was not going to help her fall asleep.

Her thoughts returned to her uncle. He was being so compassionate and generous, and yet it felt strange, uncomfortable even, that she had no clue he was so wealthy. His wealth didn't make her think more or less of him, but the Daddy-Warbucks lifestyle really shocked her. She wasn't prepared to meet a house full of staff. There was actually an upstairs housekeeper and a downstairs housekeeper. Who lives like that? Her uncle, apparently.

She knew he felt responsible for her. He always had, though she didn't really understand why. Probably because her parents were gone so much. She was a competent, grown adult, but she knew he loved her parents too and was feeling that loss. He obviously wanted to help, to *do* something. Her agreeing to stay at the ranch for a while seemed to appease him.

And truthfully, as able as she was, she really had no desire to stay alone in Austin right now. She didn't have any close friends there, mainly because she'd moved around so much since college. Well, that and her trust issues, which were well-founded. But she didn't want to think about that—then she'd *really* never fall asleep.

Staying with Marsten felt more like home than anything else, even though she'd never once visited any of his residences until this week. Home isn't a place, she reminded herself—home is wherever your family is. And Marsten was family.

Her new condo in College Station would be ready in two months, and by then her uncle should be fine. She would only be thirty minutes from his ranch. It was a coincidence her new job would be in such close proximity to her uncle. She was glad it worked out that way, and she was looking forward to using this time to get to know him better.

Her mind drifted to Jack. And their walk through the garden. She allowed her thoughts to linger around Jack McKerrick for a few minutes before she reminded herself that she didn't really know much about him. He grew up in College Station, attended Texas A&M as a member of the Corps and served as an Army Ranger. She respected and admired his service, but there were more things she didn't know about Jack than things she did know.

Sure, he seemed kind and patient. Intelligent and compassionate. But...

Head of security or not, she needed to maintain her guard. Whether to protect her physical safety, or her heart, she learned it's best to keep her walls up. High and fortified.

She'd started constructing those walls at light speed after the first kidnapping. And life had only taught her to continue to reinforce those barriers.

Except once. Briefly.

She met Neal in college. The first few dates went well. She felt so safe and comfortable with him. She decided she could be herself with him, let him in, be honest. That had been a mistake. She told him everything one evening, about her relation to the Alesi family, about the kidnappings, and the outcome. She would never forget the look on his face. Like she was a criminal.

Their relationship ended that night.

And the walls went back up. Stronger and higher than ever before.

And now, she was baffled at how quickly she considered easing her defenses around her uncle's head of security. She needed to pump the brakes, because something deep inside her wanted to trust him. And that notion was more than a little terrifying.

Her thoughts about Jack evaporated at the recognition of strange sounds near her room—very near her room.

Shuffling, creaking.

It wasn't coming from the hallway. Or her bathroom. A little louder now. A scuffling noise.

More creaking. Was it *in* her room?

No—it was *under* the house. She stared in the direction of the noises. She could hear someone clearly now—labored breathing, a whispered curse, a soft clang of metal. *There was someone under her floor.*

A tapping sound. Scraping.

She couldn't breathe. Couldn't move.

A floorboard near her bed creaked. She stared toward the sound, fear rolling through her. She watched the floorboard pop up into the room and saw fat fingers shove it to the side.

Too scared to scream, she flew out of bed, grabbed her robe and ran down the hall without looking back.

She wasn't sure where she was running. Should she wake her uncle? Had she really seen what she saw? Was she losing her mind? She found herself near the front door. *What? I made a wrong turn.* Trembling, she fumbled with her robe in the dark foyer. Why couldn't she get the robe on? Was it twisted or something? Oh, forget it. She needed to get help. She bolted for the dark hallway, trying to remember where her uncle's bedroom was and ran straight into something solid that gripped her arms.

She screamed.

It took her a few seconds to process the gentle voice trying to calm her in the darkness.

"Hey, are you okay? It's me. It's Jack."

"What?" She finally registered who he was, and relief washed over her.

"Sorry. Didn't mean to startle you. Are you okay? You set off some of the motion sensors."

"What?"

"At night, I turn on several motion sensors.

You set them off. *Are you okay?*" he asked for the third time.

"No, I'm not. There's something, *someone*, under my room. They're trying to come up through the floor!"

He tried not to look at her like she was delusional. She had a rough week, probably resulting in a nightmare. He should have expected this—the events of the past few days triggering nightmares. He understood how easily they surfaced, all too well.

"Okay. I doubt that's what you heard, but I'll check it out."

"Does the house have a basement?" she asked, still breathless. "That's what it sounded like. Like someone was in the basement under my room."

He heard the fear in her voice. "Hey, it's okay. Don't worry, I'll check it out." She was trembling. And he couldn't stand it. He wrapped his arm around her. He didn't want to behave unprofessionally, but she was shaking like a leaf, ridiculously twisted up in her robe in the middle of the night worried about the boogey man literally under her bed. His gut twisted when he registered the terror in her eyes. He understood fear. He rubbed her arm, fighting the urge to pull her tight against him until she stopped shaking. "You'll be fine. I promise. I'll go check your room. But no, there's no basement."

"I know what I saw. There's someone under my floor. They pried up one of the floorboards, I saw their fingers."

Wow. She was adamant. He walked her down the hall, sensing it best not to argue.

"Do you have your gun with you?" she asked.

"What?"

"Your weapon. Maybe you should go get it."

He didn't respond. He didn't know how.

He could hear her fear in every word. It was killing him. But no way did he think someone was under the house. He had security cameras with motion sensors all over the property now. Even if someone had tried to get under the house, they'd set off the cameras first.

Unless it was some kind of critter. That was possible. Deer had set off the cameras a few times, but it was feasible that a raccoon could get by a camera without being detected.

He didn't want to hope she'd had a nightmare, but he also didn't want to battle a raccoon. Raccoons are mean.

Brynnan grabbed his arm to get his attention when they neared the doorway. 'Be quiet,' she mouthed silently. He watched her strain her eyes in the darkness as she peered into the bedroom. She wordlessly indicated they should move slowly. She was taking this very seriously.

Jack changed his mind about hoping she'd had a dream. Now he was hoping he would find something, even if it was a raccoon. He couldn't bear to tell her she was imagining things. He was getting the impression that conversation wouldn't go well.

He crept into the room, feeling a little ridiculous. He listened for a minute. Finally, he whispered, "I'm going to turn the light on. Whatever it was, I think it's gone."

He flicked on the light. She stood about two feet from him, looking disheveled and confused, her eyes still adjusting to the light.

"I'm sorry, Brynnan. I think maybe it could've been—"

Brynnan's hands flew to her mouth. She stared in horror at something behind him, all color drained from her face.

He spun around half expecting an armed attacker lunging for him. But there was no one. And then he saw it. Four wood planks of the flooring beside her bed had been removed. Thankful he'd grabbed his cell phone on the way out of his room, he took it out and turned on the flashlight.

He laid on the floor, shone the flashlight into the opening, and carefully stuck his head into the hole to get a better look. "Gun!" he yelled and shoved his body away from the opening with so much force he nearly barreled into Brynnan.

A deafening gunshot sounded under the floorboards.

In one fluid motion, Jack grabbed Brynnan around the waist and practically carried her into the hallway.

"Come with me. Stay close," he ordered.

They ran to his room, Jack calling 911 on their way. His words were quick, and much calmer than Brynnan thought she would've been capable of in the moment. When they entered his room, he ended the call, grabbed his gun, and ran back into the hall, pausing briefly to make sure she was following.

"Where are we going?"

In a few short strides he unlocked a door and pulled her inside. "Here," he said.

She wanted to ask where 'here' was, but he already had his cell up to his ear again on another call. He ran to a cluster of glowing computer monitors. He stared at the screens, clicking on a keyboard. Brynnan realized he was looking at the security camera feeds from around the property. Apparently, they were standing in the security office.

She looked around for a light switch.

Jack must have read her mind. "Don't turn the lights on. I have no idea where that guy is, but I don't want to advertise where we are." He still held his phone to his ear with one hand.

"Who are you calling?"

"Your uncle. He's not answering." He ended the call. "There's nothing on the cameras. I need to know what's under this house and how to access it." He moved toward the door. "Stay here. Lock the door behind me. Don't let anyone in but me, understand?"

Brynnan could tell he was in full soldier mode, but he was out of his mind if he thought she was going to stay in here by herself. "*Are you kidding?* Whoever shot at you was coming up *through the floor*, not through a door! I'm not any safer in here than in my room. I'm coming with you."

The second the words were out of her mouth she realized she didn't know where he was planning on going. She didn't want to be on the front lines chasing down the shooter, but she thought she was probably safer with Jack, and his gun, than anywhere by herself, unarmed. He seemed to be considering the same thing.

"Fine. Come on," he said. He grabbed her hand and rushed her out the door.

Running back through the dark hallways, she wasn't sure why he was holding her hand this time. Possibly to keep her moving at his pace. It was working.

It also helped calm her.

She realized, again, she didn't know where they were running to, but before she could ask, they burst into Marsten's bedroom.

Marsten was already wearing his robe and putting on his slippers. "What's going on? I heard something that sounded like a gunshot."

"Yes, sir, that's exactly what you heard," said Jack. "I tried to call you."

"I leave my phone on silent at night. What's going on?"

Jack relayed everything and then launched into his questions. "Sir, you told me earlier there was no sub-floor to this house, but there is obviously something beneath the house. Do you know where the entrance is? Whoever was down there probably took off. I think they fired off a shot just to keep me from following. They might be long gone by now, but I need to check it out."

Brynnan finally realized her robe was a tangled mess. While her uncle answered, she wrangled out of it and quickly slipped it back on, correctly.

"No, no, there's nothing. That doesn't make any sense. Are you sure?" Marsten looked baffled.

"Yes, sir. I can show you what I found in Brynnan's room, but first, are you positive you don't know of any access under the house?"

"No, I don't, I—" Something akin to disbelief flashed across his face.

"What is it?"

"Well," Marsten said, "I can only think of one possibility."

"What?" Brynnan and Jack responded in

unison.

Marsten grabbed a flashlight. "Come. I'll show you. It's my best guess."

They stepped into the hallway, nearly running into Buck. And his shotgun.

Jack looked relieved. "Glad to see you, Buck."

"I heard a shot."

"I know. We're checking it out. Will you check on the rest of the staff? And tell them to stay in the house. I'm pretty sure the shooter is outside at this point."

He didn't offer more explanation, and Buck didn't seem to need any—as if taking orders on a routine mission. Nothing rattled Buck.

Marsten took off for the front door with Jack at his heels. Brynnan was glad Jack didn't try to leave her with Buck. He hadn't said anything to her during the exchange, so she stuck close and followed Jack and Marsten out of the house.

She couldn't rationalize why she felt safe with Jack. But an armed intruder had just tried to break into her bedroom, so this was no time to analyze her feelings. Her gut said staying with Jack was a good call, and until her adrenaline abated enough for her to think straight, she'd just go with her gut.

On the way out of the house, Marsten explained that when he and his cousins were boys, they spent several weeks at the ranch one summer. They enjoyed exploring the extensive property. At some point they discovered an underground tunnel system that ran from the stables to the greenhouse and to one of the guest houses. There were many branches to the underground maze, but they were partially caved in. As boys, they told themselves these other branches were too dangerous to explore, but Marsten knew they were all a little afraid of the long, dark tunnels.

"We wondered if any of the underground passages ran under the main house, but like I said, we never had the courage to go that far. That was so long ago. I might have been eleven or twelve. I didn't return to the ranch until I was in college. I never looked for the tunnels again. I would have mentioned them to you, Jack, had I remembered."

"I know, sir."

They were standing outside now. Marsten started directing them to the greenhouse.

"Wait a minute, sir. You said you know of three entrances?"

"Yes, the only ones I know of are the greenhouse, the second guest house and the stables. I can show you."

Jack shook his head. "No. Not right now anyway. Change of plans." He waved them back toward the house, walking so quickly they could barely keep up.

"What are we doing?" asked Brynnan.

"We don't know where he is, which entrance he used, or whether or not he's alone. We *do know* he's armed. I don't want to go searching in the dark like this. One thing we can assume is that he didn't walk to this ranch. There's a drone with night vision in the security office. I'm going to look for his car. I can also check the cameras around the property and the perimeter from my office again. He should've set off at least one motion detector trying to access the property, but he didn't. I'm going to figure out why." He held open the front door for Marsten and

Brynnan as they re-entered the house.

Neither Brynnan nor Marsten had any interest in going back to bed, so they waited for the police in the security office.

Jack was back outside with the drone up and running almost immediately. The intruder had a significant jump-start on his escape, but Jack knew the main house sat about a half mile from the road. He figured someone couldn't run full out in the old tunnels that probably turned a few times under the property, or so he hoped.

He hadn't practiced with this particular drone before, but what he was trying to do wasn't complicated. The ranch sat twenty miles from any semblance of civilization. And it was after two o'clock in the morning. If he spotted any vehicle, or any human being at all, they would be suspicious.

It didn't take long. Not far from the front gate, a dark vehicle was parked on the opposite side of the road. He hovered the drone closer to get a better look. Initially, he thought the plan was a long shot. Now he was seeing a lot more than he expected. And he was calling the police. Again.

CHAPTER FOUR

By the time the sun came up the state troopers were finishing up their report at the ranch. They'd stopped the intruder ten minutes after Jack lost sight of him with the drone. Marsten filed charges.

Mora helped Brynnan move all her things into a different guest room and Annalee started breakfast early, since the whole house was awake. Everyone could hear the state troopers' vehicles making their exit on the gravel drive when Marsten and Jack finally joined the rest of the household in the kitchen.

Marsten approached Brynnan, looking as worried about her as he did the night her parents died, if not more so. "Sweetheart…" He took both her hands in his. "I know it didn't seem so last night, but from now on, I promise, you are safe here." She saw raw pain in his eyes mixed with fierce concern, and regret. It was a familiar look. She'd seen it twice before. She hated that she caused her uncle that kind of worry and pain. Again. Last night hadn't been anything compared to before. Surely, he understood that. But he was probably afraid last night would resurrect painful memories and buried fears. He might be right.

"Please don't worry about me. I'll be fine. I know I'm safe here." She gave him a hug. "I'll be fine, really."

"You always are. You're strong. I just worry."

"Please don't."

Marsten smiled. "Well, promise me you'll get some sleep today. I know you didn't get any rest last night."

"I will," she promised. And sent up a silent prayer. *Please, Lord, keep the nightmares away. I've come so far. Please don't let last night pull me back under.*

Marsten turned his attention to the rest of the household staff whispering amongst themselves in the kitchen. "I'm sorry about all the disturbance this morning. The tunnels under this property will be secured and monitored. Mr. McKerrick will see to that today. The safety of everyone here is my highest priority. If any of you have any concerns about your safety, now or in the future, please don't hesitate to bring your concerns to Mr. McKerrick or myself. I take full responsibility for the tunnels not being secure. Their existence was a faint boyhood memory that I failed to report to Mr. McKerrick. For those of you who didn't get much sleep last night, feel free to take the morning off. Personally, I'm going to take a nap." He downed some orange juice, gave a forced, weary smile to his staff and turned to leave.

"A word please," he said quietly, as he passed Jack.

Jack followed him down the hall and into his

study.

"Shut the door," Marsten said.

Jack obeyed.

Marsten ran his hands over his face, looking older than usual. "I really am going to get some sleep soon, and so should you."

Jack started to say something and Marsten held up his hand. "Yes, I know. We need to talk to Brynnan about what you saw. She needs to know. But she didn't sleep at all last night. I don't think it's the best time. This afternoon will be soon enough. You need sleep too."

"Sir, I'm accustomed to going without sleep. I'm going to see to those tunnels first. Until we have them sealed, or locked, or however you wish to deal with them, I'm going to install some motion activated cameras in and around them. And I'll block off the known entrances. I'm sure Buck can help me with that."

"Yes," Marsten nodded, "that sounds good."

"I'll see you this afternoon sir, when you think Brynnan is feeling up to discussing this."

Marsten held up his hand. There was more on his mind.

"One more thing," Marsten's voice sounded different.

"Yes?"

"Were you in Brynnan's room when she heard the intruder?"

"Yes, I heard him, and briefly saw him, before he fired the shot, like I told the police."

Marsten gave Jack a look he couldn't decipher, but he didn't like it.

"I mean," Marsten continued, "when she first

heard the sounds, were you with her then?"

"When she first...? Wait, you mean, was I in her room at two o'clock in the morning, before all this started? *No sir,* I wasn't."

"Okay," Marsten held up his hands in surrender. "I had to ask. I guess you know Annalee is trying to push you two together."

This is insane. Did he really just say that? "Yes, sir, I'm aware." *I just didn't know you were.*

"And?"

Jack was speechless for a beat. This was beyond awkward. Marsten didn't seem to care. He was clearly comfortable in his candidness.

"Sir, I'm not sure what you're asking me."

"I'm asking if you're interested in her. I wouldn't necessarily disapprove if you were. Obviously, I trust you implicitly with my life, but when it comes to Brynnan...Brynnan is an extraordinary young woman. So, if you're looking for a summer fling, I advise you look elsewhere. I wouldn't suspect you of the type to mistreat women in any way, but I've been surprised before." He squinted at Jack like he was searching his soul. "If you decide to pursue Brynnan, you better know what you're doing."

If it was humanly possible for a person to convey profound encouragement and deadly threats at the same time, Marsten just pulled it off. He seemed to like the idea of them together—unless it went badly, then he'd get fired. Or shot.

"I understand, sir, but my main focus right now is keeping you and her safe. I have a bad feeling about that guy under the property last night. I'm keeping the lines of communication as open as I can with the police and the FBI. We'll get this figured out. I'm hoping *this* intruder will talk."

"Thank you, Jack."

"Yes, sir." Jack turned to leave.

"Try to get some rest before we bring the details from last night to Brynnan," said Marsten.

"Yes, sir."

Walking back down the hall, processing the whole situation, he tried to wrap his head around the 'extraordinary' Brynnan Marsh. She'd suffered terrifying trials and devastating loss, yet she remained kind and strong in her faith. Many people would've become bitter, but there was a warmth about her. A warmth that lit something inside him.

Jack harbored no doubts his boss enjoyed interrogating him about Brynnan. And he was sure Marsten didn't miss the fact that Jack didn't deny an interest.

But it was still a bad idea. Maybe.

Either way, last night's intruder just added to his responsibilities. For her sake, he should probably push his feelings aside and focus on *protecting* Brynnan. *That* he could do. He'd protect her with everything he had.

Brynnan woke up from her much needed nap around mid-afternoon. She was grateful, and surprised, she'd slept as well as she did. The nightmares hadn't returned. She was afraid the tormenting dreams inspired by her kidnappers might return her after her scare last night. She'd made so much progress—come so far in recent years. Maybe they were gone for good. She hoped so. She especially didn't want to wake up in a cold sweat, screaming at the top of her lungs in her uncle's home. She didn't want him to see her like that. Didn't want Jack to see that side of her. Or anyone for that matter.

She did feel safer in the new guest room she moved into that morning. Her uncle claimed there was no tunnel under this room, but she knew there was no way he could really be sure of that yet. However, since she'd been told last night's intruder was arrested, and her uncle and Jack assured her she was safe, she submitted to her exhaustion and slept soundly for several hours.

She showered, dressed, and then, feeling much more human than the night before, she wandered into the kitchen looking for something to eat. She was starving.

"Oh, sweetheart, you're up! How are you feeling?" Annalee hovered over her, concern all over her face.

"I'm fine, Annalee, really."

"You must be hungry. What would you like? I have some chicken salad made up. There's some brisket in the frig and some fruit salad. Or would you like me to make you an omelet? I have—"

"Don't go to any trouble, please. Chicken salad sounds wonderful."

"Oh, of course. You just sit here. I'll make you a plate. Did you get enough sleep?"

"Yes, I feel much better. Is everyone else up?"

"I haven't seen Mr. Kade yet. Jack came in to get something to eat about eleven this morning. I don't think he'd gotten any sleep yet. Bless his heart, such a rough start to this new job. He was very busy all morning doing whatever he was doing about those tunnels." She turned to the door and smiled. "Well, your ears must've been burning. I was just telling Brynnan you've been busy most of the day. Did you ever get any sleep?"

Jack smiled. "Enough."

She caught him eying Brynnan's afternoon snack. "Jack, sit down. I'll make you a plate. You want some tea?"

"Yes, thank you, Ma'am." He looked at Brynnan. "How are you?"

She finished a bite of chicken salad and smiled. "Much better. I still can't believe what happened last night. It's so crazy."

Annalee started rinsing something in the sink, and Brynnan leaned close to Jack's ear. "If you have theories...not in front of Annalee," she whispered.

He nodded. He already assumed she wouldn't want to discuss the growing list of threats in front of Annalee.

Annalee handed Jack a heaping plate of chicken salad and fruit. "Here you are. Oh, let me get you some crackers too."

"Thank you, this looks delicious."

"Oh, of course darlin', you're very welcome. I'm just sorry you have your hands so full of this awful business so soon after coming to work for Mr. Kade. Coming up through the floor like that, I just can't believe it." She added an assortment of crackers to his plate. "Of course, a lot of criminals are just plain crazy. I watch the news. And we've had a few loonies over the years try to get at Mr. Kade or some of his things. One time, at a party back at the house in

Houston, a guest actually pocketed Mr. Kade's watch and several other guests' jewelry from the pool area while they were swimming! When security confronted him with his pockets still full of the loot, the little thief looked like he was going to wet himself. He gave everything back, but I just couldn't believe the nerve."

Jack smiled at the story. He wished last night's attempt had been as simple and straightforward as snatching a watch.

Annalee busied herself with cleaning the kitchen while Jack and Brynnan enjoyed their meal.

They made some small talk, but Brynnan looked like she had questions she didn't want to ask in front of Annalee.

He wanted to assure her they could talk soon. "Your uncle and I are going to discuss everything that happened last night in a few minutes in his office. Would you mind joining us? We'd appreciate your input."

"Sure, of course, but I don't think I can offer you anything I didn't tell you last night." Remembering last night, she looked at Jack with 'I-told-you-so' in her eyes.

"What's that for?"

"Oh, it's just, I know how frazzled I must've looked last night. I know I screamed when you found me—I panicked, but…" She squinted at Jack. "*you* didn't believe me at first, did you?"

Jack held up his hands in surrender, the corner of his mouth tweaking up. "I confess. And apologize. You have to admit, it sounded unbelievable at the time. I assumed you'd had a bad dream, which would have been perfectly understandable."

"Apology accepted. And I wish it *had* been a

dream." She walked her empty plate to the kitchen sink. "What time are you meeting in Marsten's study?"

"One thirty."

She looked at her watch. "Oh, that's in just a few minutes. Ok, I'll meet you there." She smiled and left the kitchen.

Jack watched her leave. When he turned around Annalee was beaming at him with mischief in her eyes.

"Don't start," he said.

"She likes you too, I can tell."

Jack just shook his head and dug into his chicken salad.

Brynnan noticed the tension in the room when she arrived at Marsten's study. Her uncle asked her to take a seat.

Jack closed the door, and briefly held her gaze. His expression was difficult to read, but she sensed he was worried about her. She knew they were here to discuss last night's incident, but something was off.

"Is something wrong? They did catch the guy from last night, right?"

Marsten nodded to Jack to take the lead.

"Yes, that's the good news. He's in custody, and we're finding out everything we can about him."

"Good," she said. "Something else is bothering you two. What is it?"

Jack took a deep breath. "I promised I'd tell

you everything, to keep you informed of all the facts."
His kept his voice soft, compassionate. She
appreciated the effort behind his tone, but she was
dreading whatever he was about to say. It was going
to be bad.

"Brynnan, the car he was driving was a black
Audi. I was afraid it was too much of a coincidence
when I saw it, so I had the police check it out. The
plates match the car they believe ran your parents off
the road."

Brynnan stilled. Her entire body froze. She
forgot to breathe.

"Wait...*what?*" She started shaking her head,
looking from Jack to Marsten and back to Jack. "That
doesn't make any...That's insane!"

Jack hated to keep talking, the look on her
face was killing him, but he had to tell her everything.
They had to get this figured out.

"The images the Austin traffic cams got of his
face weren't perfect, but they match well enough. His
name is Nick Nesser. He has a record. He was
convicted of aggravated assault and breaking and
entering a few years ago. Other than that, we don't
know much. Not employment history, nothing. We
have his mug shot," he said, tapping on a laptop on
Marsten's desk and turning it to face Brynnan. "Do
you recognize him at all?"

She leaned forward and studied the hardened
face on the screen. "No, he doesn't look familiar. I
don't think I've ever seen him before."

Jack wasn't surprised, but he was hoping for a
clue.

He wasn't finished with his news. Maybe he
should've kept talking—delivered all the implications

in one breath—like ripping off a bandage.

"And," he waited for her to look at him, "he called the same lawyer as the shooter in Austin."

He watched the color drain from her face. She was speechless. And frightened.

Jack looked at Marsten.

Marsten took his cue and cleared his throat. "I know the lawyer. I haven't used him myself, but I know of him. His name is Mitch Kandle. He's very…exclusive."

"What does that mean?" asked Brynnan.

Before pushing the truth forward, Jack paused to send up a prayer. *Please help her through this. Soften the blow.*

"It means he's extremely expensive. He only works for people in certain circles of money and influence. Which means," he said as gently as possible, "Nick Nesser and the shooter in Austin were most likely hired by someone."

"What?" Brynnan shook her head. "That doesn't make any sense. Why would—" She stopped. Jack saw the realization hit her. The dots connecting.

Her choked whisper was barely audible. "You think my parents were murdered. By a hired assassin."

Jack thought he'd prepared himself for her reaction, but he hadn't come close. The hurricane of emotion on her face twisted a kind of pain inside him he'd never felt before. Not even in combat. This was different. The only thing he was spared was not having to say the words himself—she figured out his suspicions on her own.

He was hoping, of all the things that had happened in the past week, that her parents' accident was the one thing that was truly a random incident.

But Nesser just proved him wrong.

"I think it's a strong possibility," he said quietly.

Marsten walked over, sat beside her, and placed his hands over hers. "We will find out who hired him, Brynnan. And they will be brought to justice. I won't rest until they are. I give you my word."

Jack knew Marsten was serious. But it was a big promise. He prayed he could help his boss keep that promise.

Brynnan lifted her head. He watched her struggle to maintain her composure, aching to rush to her. Hold her.

Her words rolled out mechanically. Unfeeling. But her eyes, welling with tears, pulsed with fear. "Did it have to do with the Alesis? Were they involved? Or someone trying to get to my grandfather?"

"You know everything we do right now," said Jack. "I'm trying to find out what I can from the FBI and the police. Like your uncle said, we *will* figure this out."

She stood, barely holding herself together. "Thank you," she said, and walked to the door. Again, her words marched out, obeying her command of composure. Unlike her eyes. "I want to help. If there's anything I can do...let me know." She didn't wait for a reply. They watched her leave.

Silence hung in the room.

Finally, Marsten cleared his throat. "Jack, I want to keep discussing how we move forward but...for now, go check on Brynnan."

Jack's head snapped to his boss. Seriously? He realized a moment ago he was ready to stop lying to himself about how deeply he felt a visceral urge to comfort her and protect her, but he hadn't planned on telling Marsten that, and he *certainly* hadn't expected Marsten to suggest he do anything about it.

"Sir?"

Marsten sighed. "I'm not the best one to... Please, go to her. Check on her. Stay with her a few minutes, if she'll let you. If you don't feel comfortable, send Annalee. But I don't want her to be alone."

"If you're sure *you* wouldn't rather check on her..."

"No. Hard to explain. Just, please..."

"Yes, sir."

Jack left before Marsten could change his mind. He knew Brynnan was scared. And he was tired of pretending he didn't care.

He knocked softly on her door. No answer. Maybe she'd gone somewhere else? No, her room was the most likely place. He knocked again. "Brynnan, it's Jack."

He heard movement in the room. The door cracked open, barely an inch. He couldn't see half her face in the slim opening, but he could tell she'd been crying.

"Brynnan, I don't want to intrude. I just want to make sure you're alright."

"I'm okay," she managed to whisper, but it was nowhere near convincing.

"Can I come in?"

She hesitated but opened the door.

He slipped in and shut the door behind him.

"I'm okay, or I will be. It's just a lot to process," she said, not making eye contact.

He stood about two feet away, wanting to comfort her. But more than apprehensive about the thought.

He ran a hand through his hair. "You don't have to pretend this isn't scary. But you're not alone. I guarantee your uncle and I will tackle this head on until whoever is responsible is brought to justice."

Her eyes were distant, unfocused. "Murdered..." she whispered.

"Hey," he said, attempting to garner her attention. *What could he say though?* She was trying to digest the fact that someone may have *hired* a man to *murder* her parents. Maybe he shouldn't have intruded. There weren't any words for something like this. None that he could fathom.

He shifted his weight. She turned to him, finally meeting his eyes. Her lip quivered.

And it was more than he could bear. *That's it.*

He stepped forward. "C'mere," he whispered, tugging her to him.

She hesitated, only for a second, then dove into his chest, wrapping her arms around his waist.

He exhaled a long breath he hadn't realized he was holding.

He could feel her heartbeat, her chest swelling with each breath. He couldn't ignore how perfectly she fit against him, like she was made for him. He smoothed her hair. "I'm so sorry, Brynnan," he said, his voice low, thick. "We'll figure this out, I promise."

After a few moments, she eased back, attempting to regain some composure.

"I'm usually more composed than this. In front of people, at least."

"I don't mind."

She looked down, searching for words.

"We're going to get justice for your parents, Brynnan. And we're going to keep you safe. I know this is drudging up some pain...from the past, but everything is different this time."

She was looking stronger, but he didn't want to leave. There was still more to discuss with Marsten though. Questions he needed to ask.

"Your uncle and I are going to keep working on this. You don't have to come back to the study, but—"

"No, I want to come." She stood straighter and pushed her hair back behind her shoulders. "I'm good. Like I said, I want to help. And," she looked at him more intently, "I want to know all the facts, or theories. Don't keep anything from me."

He was relieved at the strength returning to her eyes, and the resolve in her voice.

"I won't. And hopefully we'll know more soon. The police here have contacted Austin PD about the Nesser connection. And," maybe he should have told her this sooner, "my dad works for the FBI. He's learning what he can on his end."

She took a step back. *Your dad?* Whoa, she looked surprised. "Why didn't you..." She closed her eyes and took a steadying breath.

"Um, I didn't realize that would upset you. Look, it's actually a good thing. We need answers. And working security for your uncle doesn't grant me a lot of privileges with law enforcement. The police have been reasonably helpful, but... Look, I know what I said in the car the other day, but I want to rule out any connection to the Alesi family. If any of this has to do with retribution to the Alesis, we need to start working with the FBI sooner rather than later."

Her head bobbed slowly. "I get it. I do. It's just... Has your dad read my file? Have you? I've worked so hard to leave all of that in the past. The thought of..."

Her voice hitched.

He felt like an idiot. She didn't mind them working with the FBI—what she didn't want was more people reading her file, knowing the gruesome details of her past. Why hadn't he realized that?

"Hey, no, I haven't read your file. I have no idea what information my dad has come across so far, but *please* understand, everything we're doing is to keep you safe."

Her innocent eyes pleaded with him.

"If you do...you need to know, I was a different person then."

"No one is judging you on your past, Brynnan. I promise. And that file might be irrelevant anyway. If anyone looks at it, it's only in an effort to keep you safe."

Her shoulders relaxed a fraction.

"Okay. Sorry. I'm not trying to be dramatic. I just hate the thought of any of that haunting me again."

"Don't apologize." He could relate. But he didn't want to dump all that on her right now.

She looked so strong and so vulnerable at the same time...he could hardly stand it. He really wished he didn't want to kiss her right now. Horrible timing. He must be out of his mind. He forced his hands to his sides and stepped back to the door.

She gave him a small smile, and he followed her out.

Marsten looked surprised, then worried, when they walked back in the study.

"I'm fine," said Brynnan. "I want to know what you're both thinking. Jack said there was more to discuss."

Marsten considered her a moment, then decided to move forward, nodding to Jack to take the lead.

"There's a lot we don't have access to, so I say we start with the resources we *do* have, to figure out what Nesser wanted and who sent him. Let's start with the tunnels. Who knows about them? That can't be a very long list."

Marsten nodded. "True. Except I don't know with certainty how many people know about them. When I was a boy, I had the impression my cousins and I were the only ones who had ventured into them in several years. At the time, my uncle, and a butler who worked in this house for many years, both knew about the tunnels. They would tease us about ghosts or monsters inhabiting the tunnels. I never learned why or when the tunnels were initially created, though I suspect my uncle and his butler knew."

"Any chance we could ask them about the tunnels now?" asked Jack.

"My uncle is in his nineties. He's living in Houston. He doesn't hear very well now and hates talking on the phone, but if it will help, I could visit him and ask."

"What about the butler?"

Marsten laughed. "Oh, no, afraid not. I was sure he was a thousand years old when I was a child, he retired years ago. I'm sure he's gone now."

"And your cousins? How many cousins knew about the tunnels? Could you ask them who they may have told?" Jack asked.

Marsten didn't respond at first. His expression turned cold. "I'll have to think about that." He looked from Jack to Brynnan, and back to Jack. Finally, he said, "I'm not so sure some of them shouldn't be suspects. They certainly have the money. And morals and ethics run pretty thin amongst most of the Kades."

Turning to Brynnan, his expression softened. "I don't know how much your father ever told you. But that's one reason he kept you and your mother away from the Kade family properties, away from my world. Your father and I got along. I dare say we were close. But he never trusted the Kade family, and I never blamed him. They're a rotten bunch. Mostly." He sighed heavily. "Now I've brought you here, and this is what's happened."

Jack saw the distress in his boss's eyes. "Sir, bringing Brynnan here may have saved her life. Staying at her parents' house alone was not a safe option." He hoped he hadn't said too much. He didn't want to scare Brynnan, but he knew he was right.

Thankfully, Brynnan nodded in agreement and gave her uncle a small smile. "I definitely feel safer here right now."

Marsten's expression softened again. "Well, like Jack said, you *are* safe here now. I promise you that." He turned to Jack. "Where do we start?"

"Sounds like we should start with your cousins."

CHAPTER FIVE

Over the next half hour, Marsten described the rather eccentric four cousins who explored the tunnels with him so many years ago. There were other relatives, he reasoned, who may know of their existence, but Jack decided to focus on the uncle and cousins who Marsten was sure knew about the various entrances to the tunnels.

"Could you call them? Feel them out? See how they react when you mention the tunnels? If they're guilty of anything, I don't expect any kind of confession, but maybe we could judge their reactions and narrow down who could possibly be involved." Jack asked.

Marsten wore a pensive expression. "I'm not sure that's the best course of action."

"Why not?" Jack asked.

Marsten searched for his words. Jack tried not to look impatient. But he was.

"It's difficult to explain the tenuous relationship I have with my cousins. But suffice it to say we might have better luck visiting them in person."

"That would be *much* more helpful in gauging their reactions, if you think they'll meet with us."

"Yes, I can make that happen. And I can't think of anyone else to question about the tunnels at this point. Besides my uncle. We can visit him last, if we think it's necessary. I'm less suspect of him, to be quite frank though."

"If you don't mind me saying so," said Brynnan "you seem suspicious of your cousins. Do you really think they're guilty of any of this? And why would they be?"

"My dear, most of the Kades are guilty of many things. We just need to determine whether any of them have a hand in *this* situation."

His accusation sounded ominous. And, once again, Jack was wondering if he should have agreed to work for a Kade. He needed to stop that line of thinking. It was pointless. Because he was in the middle of this, and he wasn't backing out now. Not until things calmed down. And he was sure Brynnan wasn't in danger. He needed to wrap up this issue with Nesser and whoever hired him. After that, he might reevaluate his career choices.

The uncle and three of the cousins lived in Houston, the fourth in Dallas. They decided it made the most sense to speak with his Houston relatives first and go from there. Marsten wanted Jack to accompany him. Whether it was decided Brynnan should go too because she'd be safer with them, or because she insisted on being involved, was unclear. Either way, the decision was made—all three would be heading to Houston the next day.

Half an hour later, the first two additions to Jack's security team arrived. Both had served with Jack in the past. He knew them well. And he knew they were looking at this as a short-term gig to make a considerable amount of money. If he wanted them to stay on for the long term, he'd have to do some convincing. Especially for his friend, Cole Hale.

Cole left the military a year ago and lived in Dallas with his wife and two kids. He'd been deployed four times and wanted to spend more time with his family. His wife and kids were very happy in Dallas and weren't looking to move, but Jack knew, while Cole was enjoying being with his family more, he wasn't happy in his current position working security for a bank. Jack was hoping the raise in pay would entice Cole to move his family and join him at Kade Ranch permanently.

The second addition, also a former teammate that he'd convinced to come onboard, was Zeke Beardall. He went by Beardall most of the time, or just 'Bear'. Because it fit him. With more hair and height than couth, well-suited nicknames like 'Sasquatch' and 'Chewbacca' had been suggested by teammates over the years, but they were deemed too long. Jack definitely wanted his hefty friend on staff at the ranch as well, but he didn't know what else Beardall had committed to lately, if anything. Ever since he left the military a few months ago, Beardall floated around the country, not staying in one place very long. Thankfully, he still paid his cell phone bill.

They were both committed until the present situation was resolved. That was good enough for Jack, for the time being.

"We'll have dinner tonight with Mr. Kade and

Brynnan," Jack explained as Cole and Beardall lugged their bags into the second guest house. "That will give Mr. Kade a chance to get to know y'all. He's big on that—wants to know all his employees well. But if you're hungry before then, Annalee always has something in the kitchen."

"Good. I'm starved," said Beardall.

"Of course, you are," said Cole. "We only stopped for food twice on our three-hour drive between Dallas and here."

"I'm a growing boy," Beardall shrugged.

"You don't need to grow any more, Bear," Cole said.

"I'm just glad you two are here," said Jack. "Get settled, and I'll show you around. Mr. Kade, Brynnan, and I will be in Houston for a few hours tomorrow. You two are the security while we're gone. We're responsible for the safety of everyone at the ranch. At present, I believe Mr. Kade and Brynnan are the highest security concerns, but don't let your guard down."

"Roger that," said Cole, admiring the furnishings in their three-bedroom guest house. "This place is incredible. And huge. How many buildings are on the property?"

"Including a greenhouse and stables, eight."

Cole let out a low whistle. "So, this is how billionaires live? This'll be interesting."

"Actually, he's a multi-billionaire, and no, I have no idea how many billions he has and no, I'm not going to ask. But I mention that because he has a few other properties I haven't seen yet, around the country and overseas. He's using this as his primary residence for now, so this ranch is our main priority."

"So..." Bear scratched his day-old beard and settled his massive frame on the oversized sectional. "Is Kade, say, Scrooge McDuck rich, or Tony Stark rich?"

"What's the difference?" asked Cole.

Leaning back and propping his feet on the coffee table, Bear formulated his response, "Well, Scrooge—"

Jack kicked his hairy friend's feet off the furniture. "I'm going to pretend you're not having this conversation."

Cole busted out with a laugh and plenty of sarcasm. "You seem stressed, pal."

"You think? We had a break-in less than a week after I started, so yeah, I'm focused right now."

This wasn't news to Cole or Beardall. Jack explained the situation when he called them.

"We know," said Cole. "But don't worry," he plopped down on the sectional and clapped Beardall on the shoulder, "the calvary's here."

"I don't do horses," said Beardall, who was probably joking, but his monotone response didn't betray any humor.

"No one wants you on a horse, Bear, *least of all* the horse," said Cole.

Beardall shrugged.

Jack had to stay focused until the entire situation was resolved, but now that Cole and Beardall were here, he actually felt less stressed. He was grateful for the help.

He relayed his entire meeting regarding the tunnels and cousins with Cole looking attentive, and Beardall trying out all the buttons on the recliner. There was a massage option. Jack wasn't sure he had

Bear's attention after that discovery.

Cole looked confused. "Why is his niece going to Houston tomorrow with you? Bear and I can keep her safe here. If there's a legitimate threat of her being kidnapped, she'd be safer here."

Jack sighed with a discomfort he hoped Cole wouldn't pick up on. "Yes, I know. We can suggest that at dinner, but I'm not going to push it. Mr. Kade is in charge here and he doesn't want to tell her 'no.' She's pretty insistent. Besides, it's not like we're taking any public transportation. We're taking his private helicopter from here to a helipad at one of his cousin's estates, then, if we decide to visit his other relatives while we're in Houston, his cousin's chauffeur will drive us."

Both men's eyebrows shot up. "Of course, he will," said Cole. "Well, don't worry, while you're flying around in Tony Stark's private chopper, we'll hold down the fort here. One question," he said holding up his index finger, "is anyone here named Jeeves?"

"Yeah," said Beardall, "please tell me there's a butler named Jeeves."

Jack glared at them. "Guys, we have a serious situation here. The ex-con responsible for Brynnan's parents' *deaths* tried to enter her room last night. This is a legitimate threat." He may have raised his voice a little more than he'd intended.

"Hey man," said Beardall, "we get it. Just messing with you."

"Yeah, Jack, we're here to work. I promised Bear this wouldn't be a babysitting job—I promised him we were coming to catch bad guys. We're on board. You're the boss, where do we start?"

Jack's phone chimed. He'd set up a security

app to send him a notification every time there was movement outside the house. It was already getting annoying. But until he had someone monitoring cameras in the security office 24/7, he needed to know everything, all the time.

He glanced at the image on his phone and saw Brynnan carrying a box to the garage. And opening one of the garage doors. *What?*

"Guys, get unpacked. I need to check on something. I'll be right back."

"Take your time," said Bear, who had now found the tv remote and, was clearly impressed with the surround sound. "We'll be just fine."

Brynnan put the cardboard box in the backseat of her 4runner and shut the door.

"What are you doing?"

The voice startled her. She spun around to face Jack's confused expression.

She caught her breath. "You scared me. I guess my nerves are still a bit frazzled."

He looked so apologetic. Oh. She didn't mean for him to feel bad. She narrowed her eyes at him with a half grin. "I never hear you coming. I guess your ninja skills are part of your Special Forces training?"

"Funny. But seriously, where are you going?"

She opened the driver's side door and tossed in her purse. "A colleague of my dad's called. He lives in the area, in Bryan. He offered to work on authenticating this box of artifacts. They were the last thing my parents were working on. I guess my dad mentioned it to him. I'm going to take the box to his house."

"You have the box here?"

Brynnan paused. How could she explain? "Like I said, it was the last thing my parents were working on. The very last thing. They had the box in their car that night. A friend picked up my parents' belongings from the car. There wasn't much. But yes, I brought it with me. I thought about working on it myself, but when he offered this morning, I thought it sounded like a better idea." She didn't want to get emotional right now. She forced a smile. "It won't take me long. I'll be back in an hour. I'm looking forward to meeting the security team you hired. Marsten said they're friends of yours, that you served with?"

"Yes, they are. You'll meet them at dinner, but back to this," he said, pointing at the 4runner. "It's not a good idea for you to be going anywhere alone right now. Not until we find out why Nesser was here last night."

Brynnan frowned. "Believe me, I probably want to know that more than you do. And I'm not trying to do anything dangerous. This man, Professor Krupp, was a friend of my father's. I don't know him well, but I've met him before. He just wanted to help finish what my parents were working on. I guess…" she diverted her eyes from his, trying to make her words sound less pitiful. "I need to *do* something. I guess I thought getting this done would be cathartic. Anyway, it won't take me long, I'll be right back."

If his face was any evidence, she hadn't done a good job convincing him she needed to deliver the box. She appreciated that ensuring her safety was part of his job but driving straight to Professor Krupp's house shouldn't put her at any risk.

"I understand, Brynnan, I do, but…" He sighed.

Apparently, she was frustrating him.

"Look, I'm not saying don't go, you just shouldn't go alone. I'll go with you."

Really? She didn't see that coming. "Umm, okay. If you want."

"Let me make sure my guys know how to monitor the security cameras first. Give me fifteen minutes?"

"Sure. I'll meet you back here."

Fifteen minutes later, Jack drove the 4runner out the front gate with Brynnan in the passenger seat looking up Professor Krupp's address.

They kept the conversation light all the way to Bryan. He learned she was a dog person. And didn't like soft drinks. She asked about his family. He talked about his brothers, and his parents' home, where he'd grown up.

"Mom has a huge vegetable garden and flower garden that she loves. So, dad's hobby is protecting her gardens from armadillos, rabbits and raccoons by all means necessary."

"That's nice of him."

Jack grinned. "Yes, it is. Dad would do anything for Mom, but really, I think he likes the challenge of keeping the yard free of critters. She kept some chickens for a while. The fresh eggs were awesome, but the chickens attracted coyotes. Mom got tired of Dad, me and my brothers shooting at them."

There was a warmth in his voice Brynnan admired, maybe envied. She sensed his family shared a closeness that she couldn't quite relate to. "Your family sounds wonderful."

She looked ahead and down at her phone. "This is it. Turn here. His house is the third one on the right."

Jack pulled onto a quiet residential street with large, well-kept yards and mature trees. He parked in the circle drive.

Brynnan unbuckled her seatbelt. "You don't need to get out. I'm not going in. I'll just hand it to him at the door. Be right back."

She was out of the car and grabbing the box from the backseat before he had a chance to reply. It was fine. The front porch was literally twenty feet away. He could keep a close eye from the driver's seat.

Brynnan rang the doorbell trying to remember what Professor Krupp looked like. It had been a few years since she'd seen him.

But when the door opened, she was sure it was him. Long hair, thick glasses, chubby middle. He didn't look any different than she remembered.

"Hello Brynnan," he said, through a stiff, unnatural smile.

"Hello, Professor Krupp. I brought the artifacts." She held up the box.

"Yes, thank you for bringing them. I'm glad to have the opportunity to authenticate them."

The hairs on Brynnan's skin stood rigid. Something was off. Professor Krupp's words made

sense, but the man looked nervous, more like terrified. He was sweating. His arm trembled.

"Are you okay?" she asked.

"Yes, yes. Just *please* come in. You can put the box in my study."

Her question agitated him. What was going on? This didn't feel right. She held on to the box.

"Everything okay?" Jack appeared next to her. *How could over six feet of pure muscle move so silently?* At the moment, she didn't care, she was just relieved he was there. Professor Krupp, however, did *not* look relieved to see Jack.

More flustered now, Professor Krupp raised his voice. Sweat poured from his temples. "Who are you? I mean, yes, yes, of course, everything is fine." Professor Krupp suddenly looked confused, like he didn't know how to process Jack's presence.

The jittery professor's eyes darted to his right, behind the partially opened front door. Apparently, whatever he saw helped him make a decision. "You can just stay out here. I mean…my house is such a mess. I…I just need Brynnan to put the box in my study. We'll be right back."

No. Way.

Jack had no idea what was going on, but he knew he wasn't letting Brynnan in that house. Jack was growing more sure Professor Krupp was under duress. From what, he didn't know, but he needed to get Brynnan back in the car. Now.

He kept his tone low and firm. "Brynnan, get in the car."

Suddenly, Professor Krupp stepped out onto the porch, his eyes wild with…desperation? Jack thought he was about to grab the box away from Brynnan, but instead, he bolted off the porch, and raced down the sidewalk, frantically fishing for something in his pockets. His car keys finally tumbled to the ground. Dropping them two more times before he successfully pressed 'unlock' on his fob, he jumped in his car, and veered down the driveway so erratically he plowed through a flowerbed and clipped his own mailbox. He sped down the street and was out of sight in seconds.

Brynnan and Jack stood on the porch dumbfounded.

"You think he's on drugs or something?" Brynnan asked.

"Okay, that was weird," said Jack.

Motion at the doorway drew their attention. A different man stood in front of them. This one wasn't sweating and wasn't scared. And he held a knife.

He pointed his weapon at Jack. "I don't care who you are. All I need is Brynnan, and that box. She's going to bring the box inside to me, and *you* are going to *leave*. Now." He held the knife in his right hand, and with his left he moved his jacket enough to show Jack he was also armed with a gun.

Mr. Krupp wasn't on drugs. He'd definitely been under duress.

Jack lifted his hands, as if surrendering. He spoke in calming tones like he was trying to soothe a spooked horse. "Whoa. Alright. We were just leaving." He eased himself between Brynnan and the man as he spoke. Not taking his eyes off the knife-wielding stranger, he lowered his voice again and repeated to Brynnan. *"Get. In. The. Car."*

She immediately started backing up.

"Hey! I said, *come inside*. With the box." He flicked his knife toward Jack. "And *you*, are going to leave. Now."

The box of artifacts? That's what all this was about? And Brynnan? Why does he want Brynnan? Jack's mind was firing on all cylinders. And some pieces were falling into place.

His first priority was keeping Brynnan safe from this guy, but he also had every intention of leaving with the box. He sized the guy up. His stance and demeanor screamed hired thug, not military-trained mercenary. He didn't look stupid though. And he had a gun.

Jack stood his ground, acting as a wall between Brynnan and the man. He continued to stare the man down while motioning Brynnan to keep moving.

Which she did. But instead of backing up straight behind Jack, she made a beeline for the car to his right, exposing herself to the man with the knife. The man growled and turned toward her. Not good.

A split second before he threw the knife in Brynnan's direction, Jack lunged himself forward. It wasn't much of a fight. Jack was faster, in better shape, and well-trained.

In the seconds it took Brynnan to rush back to the porch, Jack had the man firmly pinned to the ground.

"You okay?" he asked her.

"Me? Yeah, sure," she answered, her voice shaky.

"Could you call 911? I have my hands full."

"Oh, yes, yes."

She pulled her phone from the back pocket of

her jeans. Her words to the operator were calm and articulate. Jack was impressed. Because he could see her hands trembling.

He asked the man several times, while they waited for the police to arrive, who he was working for, why he wanted the artifacts, and why he wanted Brynnan, but the man never spoke a word.

Soon, sirens approached, and their attacker was arrested. Jack and Brynnan were asked to wait around for a few more minutes. The police had plenty of questions for them.

Brynnan noticed a trickle of blood running down Jack's arm.

"Jack...you're hurt!"

He smudged away the few drops of blood with his hand and smiled. "It's nothing. His knife grazed me a bit. I'm fine. Are *you* okay?" His eyes searched hers with an intensity that surprised her. She didn't mind though. She was beyond grateful he was there. What if she'd come by herself? How would things have turned out? She shut her eyes, pushing away all the 'what-ifs.'

"Yes. I guess. Yes." She shook her head.

She felt Jack's gaze burrow past the composure she was trying to force onto her face, his eyes reading her mind. "Everything's going to be okay. We'll solve this. I promise."

Jack's words and nearness calmed her. *And* elicited a swarm of butterflies in her stomach.

Oh, boy.

She pressed her hands to her face. "This doesn't make sense. I've looked through the artifacts, and I didn't notice anything of exceptional value. I'm going to call my uncle. I'm going to ask why someone would want those artifacts so badly. He was the one who sent them to my parents. I'm afraid he won't know though—because, like I said, this doesn't make sense."

Jack slid his phone from his pocket. "I need to call him anyway. He needs to be updated on this. I'll ask him about the artifacts."

Confusion clouded her mind for a fraction of a second. For some reason she'd forgotten Jack was her uncle's head of security. Of course, he would need to report the attack to his boss. Because that was the only reason he was with her at Professor Krupp's in the first place. It was his job. And nothing more. She needed to remind herself of that.

That would be so much easier if she couldn't read the worry in his eyes. Concern for her radiated off of him. Yes, he was her uncle's head of security, but she knew he never looked at Marsten the way he looked at her. Never stood so close.

Oh God, why does Jack McKerrick make me feel so safe? That's wrong, isn't it? I hardly know him. I shouldn't trust him, should I? Help me to only trust you.

Jack called Marsten, and just as Brynnan predicted, he seemed genuinely shocked at the interest in the artifacts he'd sent to his brother. He claimed he had no idea they were of exceptional value, but then, he really didn't know much about their worth, which was why he'd sent them to Brynnan's father.

"Where did the artifacts come from,

originally?" asked Jack.

"Actually," Marsten paused, "they belonged to my cousin, Victor."

"One of your cousins who knows about the tunnels?"

"Yes. I don't see how it could all be connected, but yes, Victor knows about the tunnels."

"We'll have several questions for him tomorrow," said Jack.

Marsten agreed.

Jack ended the call and related the conversation to Brynnan.

She ran her fingers through her long hair, uncertainty dimming the light he'd seen in her eyes on the way over.

"I've looked at those artifacts briefly, when my parents first received the boxes. It doesn't make sense that any of those things would be worth all this," she said, gesturing to all the emergency vehicles still parked in front of Professor Krupp's house.

"Boxes? You said 'boxes,' were there more than just the one?"

Brynnan's brows shot up, her eyes impossibly wide. "Oh, good grief! I didn't think about it until just now, but yes, there were *two* boxes my parents were taking over to Professor Drummond's house the night…of the accident. But when my friend delivered the items from the car, there was only one box. She said she got everything. She couldn't have overlooked a box."

"Are you sure?"

"Yes, one hundred percent. I just hadn't really thought about the boxes until today. Like I said, my brain was in a fog for a while, and I didn't know the boxes were important until just now."

Brynnan's face looked tortured. He knew she was piecing the facts together, realizing her parents were likely killed for the contents of the box.

Her voice trembled. "They *were* murdered. It's true. They may have been murdered for those artifacts…" She shuddered.

He ached to protect her from the pain she was reliving. He slipped his hand into hers. Not his first choice. But there were still several police officers standing a few feet away, so... With a gentle squeeze, he ran his thumb across the back of her hand. She looked up at him, the tenderness and hope in her gaze cutting all the way through to parts of him he didn't know existed.

She could've asked for anything in the world in that moment, and he'd give it to her.

And just like that, all his resolve to keep things professional between them started to evaporate.

Before he could put any words to his thoughts, a police officer, with the worst possible timing, walked up. Jack tried not to glare at the guy. He was just doing his job. And the sooner they got all the questions over with, the sooner they could leave. And that was just fine with him.

He was anxious to take Brynnan back to the ranch where he felt better equipped to keep her safe.

After they told the police everything they could, Jack and Brynnan finally climbed into the 4runner. Jack started the engine, got the AC going, then pulled out his phone. He texted his dad a short update. And prayed the FBI could offer him some clues soon.

When they pulled off Professor Krupp's street, Brynnan eyed the blood on Jack's right arm. Again.

"It's fine. It looks worse than it is," he assured her.

Her eyes clearly conveyed she was not satisfied with his answer. "Okay. I understand you not wanting to go in the ambulance for it, but it's still bleeding some. Pull over, and I'll clean it," she started digging in her tote bag. "I have a small first aid kit."

"No, really, it's fine. We need to get back."

She didn't look happy. She looked at the bloody graze again. "Well, if you don't care about your arm, at least let me bandage it so you won't keep getting blood on my car."

That got his attention. He looked down. There were three drops of blood on the car seat. Not a huge deal, but it wasn't his car.

"Okay. We'll just get the bleeding stopped."

He pulled into a gas station parking lot and parked at the far end, but kept the engine running— they needed the AC. Brynnan pulled the first aid kit from her bag and went to work.

Her touch was gentle. And though his 'injury' was hardly a scratch, he appreciated her concern. He couldn't keep his eyes off her face while she cleaned his wound. She was beautiful. But what drew him to her more than that was her compassion and kindness, the intelligence in her eyes. *Whoa.* He needed to stop—for now. He wasn't going to lie to himself about his feelings for her, but if he didn't stifle these feelings right now, he was going to end up trying to kiss her before they got back to the ranch.

But her proximity to him, and her touch, were making that extremely difficult. He should stop staring at her. He shut his eyes.

"Oh, I'm sorry, did I hurt you?"

He laughed. "No. It doesn't hurt. Just tired." Okay, that sounded lame, but what was he supposed to say?

She finished securing the bandage and looked up at him, unshed tears in her eyes.

"Hey, whoa, what's wrong?"

She shook her head and blinked away the tears. "This shouldn't have happened. I shouldn't have even come. You were right, I should have stayed at the ranch. You got hurt because of me."

"Brynnan, it's really noth—"

"I know, I know," she said, waving away his words. "You're a macho soldier, and it's just a scratch, you probably never feel pain…" Now she was sounding sarcastic.

"Nope, never," he said, giving her a smile he hoped would end this guilt trip she was sending herself on.

She narrowed her eyes at him. "But it still happened. And if I'd kept backing up instead of running to the other side of the car, he wouldn't have had a chance to…"

And the tears were back.

He grabbed her hand. "None of this is your fault. And as much as I hate that you were put in danger this afternoon, we learned something very important. If we hadn't come, we still wouldn't have a clue what was going on, but now we know the attacks have something to do with the artifacts your parents were working on when they died. And the police also have a third guy in custody now who is mixed up in this. He may talk more than Nesser, or the shooter in Austin. We're a lot closer to solving this thing than we were this morning."

She swiped away the moisture under her eyes with her free hand. "I'm definitely relieved to have some clue about all this. As soon as we get back, I'm going to start combing through those artifacts. I can't imagine what could be worth all this trouble."

Jack backed out of the parking spot. "I was thinking the same thing."

"I guess, since the artifacts came from Marsten, this probably has nothing to do with the Alesi family after all, does it?"

"Doesn't seem as likely." He glanced her way and pulled back onto the highway. "I understand bringing up the possible Alesi connection was difficult for you, and I'm sorry for that, but I'm glad I know."

"Why?"

"Because I want to keep you safe. Knowing all possible threats helps me do that."

She nodded slowly. She was trying to figure out this man. *Was he simply doing his job, or did he want her safe because he cared?* She didn't think he was acting solely as professional security when he held her earlier today, or when he held her hand an hour ago, or a minute ago.

Did she want him to care? That idea was almost as scary as the man with the knife, or the shooter. Maybe more so. That sounded ridiculous, even in her mind, but she knew exposing her heart to anyone, opening herself up again, would take more courage than facing any kind of threat.

She didn't need to worry about any of that though—if he cared about her, why would he say he was glad he knew about her relation to the Alesi crime family? That would be relationship kryptonite. And if that didn't do it, he would never be interested in her after finding out the details of her kidnappings. He hadn't read her file. There were things he didn't know. And no one needed someone with that much baggage. She needed to accept that.

She noticed the way he looked at her earlier. Should she force some distance between them? Is that really what she wanted?

No. Yes. No. Oh, good grief.

Dear Lord, please grant me wisdom. Help me see your direction.

CHAPTER SIX

As soon as they returned to Kade Ranch, Jack and Brynnan debriefed Marsten on the entire incident at Krupp's house. He was relieved they were both safe.

"The box of artifacts? That's what they were after? I can't believe it." He looked at Brynnan. "You've seen those artifacts. You know more about these things than I do, why are they so valuable?"

Brynnan's shoulders sagged. "I have no idea. I'll look at them again. Do I have time before dinner?"

"Annalee is setting the table now. And you two look like you need a break. Come, sit, eat. We can look through the box after dinner."

She was anxious to get started on the artifacts, but inwardly she was relieved at his suggestion. She was hungry. And thirsty. And she wanted a little more time to process their eventful afternoon before focusing all her concentration on the artifacts.

"Sounds good to me," said Jack. "I'll check in with Cole and Beardall and meet you in a few minutes."

Jack entered the security office and found Beardall monitoring the cameras. "Hey, everything go okay this afternoon?"

"All quiet here. How was your errand? I thought you'd be back earlier."

"Jack," Cole called, rushing into the room. "Are you alright? Annalee said you were attacked."

Bear straightened his hefty frame. "What?"

"I'm fine. We're both fine." Jack sank into one of the leather desk chairs and filled them in on all the details.

Cole let out a low whistle. "Glad you decided to tag along." He glanced at Jack's bandage. "Annalee said the guy with the knife got your arm. Let me take a look."

Of the three of them, Cole had the most medical knowledge and training.

Jack tried to wave him off. "No, it's nothing. We need to meet Marsten and Brynnan for dinner."

"Hang on, it'll just take me a second." He pulled off the edge of the bandage Brynnan had applied. Both eyebrows shot up.

"What?" asked Beardall. "Is it bad?"

"Uh, no. It's not," Cole answered. He gave Jack a perplexed look. "What is this?"

"I *told you*, it's nothing."

"I thought you were trying to be all macho or something. There's almost nothing here. Did it even bleed?"

Beardall walked around to get a better look.

"Are you sure it was a knife? Looks like his fingernail grazed you."

"Very funny," Jack said, ripping off the bandage.

"Wait," said Cole, his mouth tweaking up, suddenly enjoying the exchange. "Annalee said Brynnan had to patch you up. Why did you have her put a bandage on this papercut?"

"It was starting to drip blood in the car," Jack started to explain.

"Uh huh, I see," said Cole, now grinning ear to ear. "By the way, I met Brynnan briefly in the hall. She's very attractive. Not sure you noticed that."

Jack glared. He prayed his face wasn't turning red. "Guys, she's our boss's niece. Let's just…" He pinched the bridge of his nose and shut his eyes. He wasn't sure what he wanted to say. He felt uncomfortable. Brynnan was knocking some cracks in the walls he'd built up around his emotions, around his heart, and his friends were already starting to see that. Wow. Things were happening too fast and nothing had really even happened.

He cleared his throat. "We need to meet Marsten and Brynnan for dinner." He walked out of the security office, ending the conversation. However awkwardly. Which he was sure, spoke volumes to Cole and Bear.

At dinner, Annalee served beef enchiladas, jalapeno cornbread, street corn salad and avocado slices. Beardall looked like a kid in a candy store. Annalee couldn't have been more pleased when he asked for seconds.

Marsten, Brynnan, Cole and Beardall all seemed equally impressed by each other. Jack was glad. That would make his job much easier. The conversation circled around everyone getting acquainted until just before dessert.

"What do the police think about the guy in the tunnel, Nick Nesser? How far have they gotten with him?" asked Cole.

"They're letting us know what they can, but that's not saying much," said Jack. "I know they're continuing to question him. They agree it seems like too much of a coincidence that the guy who caused Brynnan's parents' accident also tried to break into her bedroom a few days later in a different part of the state, but so far, his lawyer isn't letting him say much. He claims he didn't realize he ran a car off the road in Austin, he says he didn't see them. And he says he was never in a tunnel under this property. He says he pulled over to stretch his legs on the side of the road last night, that's all."

"Smart," said Cole. "He only copped to what the police could prove. His car was in Austin, and his car was here."

"That's about it. However, we did find out a few minutes ago that the guy with the knife called the same lawyer, Mitch Kandle, as soon as they got to the police station."

"So, it *is* all connected," said Cole.

Jack exchanged a look with Brynnan. "I never doubted it was, but yes, I'm positive they were hired by the same person."

Jack knew they needed to figure out why someone was taking such dangerous and deadly measures to obtain Marsten's box of artifacts, and why the guy with the knife seemed interested in Brynnan. He was relieved when Annalee announced dessert was on the way though—not because he thought he could eat any more or should—but he could use a short reprieve from discussing Marsten and Brynnan's safety.

Brynnan had smiled several times during dinner, even laughed at his and Cole's self-deprecating attempts at humor. He enjoyed seeing her more relaxed. Enjoyed her sweet smile. He wondered if he'd ever have the courage to tell her what her smile did to him.

Annalee brought out warm slices of chocolate chili cake and offered ice cream and coffee. As he'd hoped, dessert brought the conversation back to Marsten and Brynnan getting to know Cole and Beardall and visa versa. Jack could tell Cole and Beardall enjoyed Annalee's cooking. Especially Beardall. He was pretty certain Bear might agree to stay on as part of his security team solely because he knew he'd eat well. It wouldn't be the worst reason to accept a job.

A few minutes later, Marsten finished his coffee and pushed back his chair. "I don't want to rush you off, but I know there's not much daylight left, and you want to look around."

"Yes," said Jack. "I'm going to show them the different buildings on the property and the entrances to the tunnels."

"Excellent. If you don't need anything else from me, I'll see you in the morning. We'll leave at nine."

"Yes, sir. Goodnight."

There was actually something else Jack wanted to

know more about, but he didn't want to bring it up to Marsten yet. He'd find it too far-fetched. When Annalee brought out the dessert earlier, it reminded him of something. And now he couldn't shake the idea. He didn't like coincidences.

CHAPTER SEVEN

Jack showed Cole and Beardall the main house, guest houses, pool house, greenhouse, stables, and all known entrances to the tunnel system, including the one across the road from the Kade property line. They ended up in Brynnan's original bedroom looking through the hole in the floor.

"These tunnels are crazy," said Cole. "What were they for?"

"I don't know," said Jack. "I'm curious, but I doubt their original use has anything to do with what's going on. I'm more interested in who hired Nesser and the guy at Krupp's house—I think the police said his name is Paul Fischer."

"Sure does seem like they were hired. You *really* have no idea who is behind this?" asked Beardall.

Jack shook his head. "I wasn't holding anything back earlier in front of Marsten and Brynnan. I really don't know. I'm definitely curious about these Kade cousins. It could be a waste of time, but it's somewhere to start. And honestly, if I'm going to keep working for Marsten, I feel like we need to know a little bit more about the rest of the Kades. I never considered any of them a threat as far as security before I took this job, but Marsten obviously doesn't trust them, so neither should we."

"Are you positive neither Nesser or Fischer is the guy behind this?" asked Cole.

"I haven't had time to look into this Fischer guy, but nothing about him said 'mastermind.' He's either a great actor or hired muscle. I did look into Nesser earlier, as much as I could, and there's no way he is paying for his lawyer himself. So, if he wasn't hired, he has an extremely wealthy friend helping him get out of trouble. The police say he only made one phone call after his arrest, and that was to this high-dollar lawyer—not to any friend or family member. And I'm convinced he's not paying this guy. So, there was a plan, 'if you get caught, call this number.' And Paul Fischer did the exact same thing—didn't call *anyone* except Mitch Kandle."

Cole nodded and looked into the cavernous space under the floorboards. "You said this happened in the middle of the night? So, Brynnan's lying in bed and hears someone coming up through her floor? She must've been really freaked out."

"Yeah, she was pretty spooked when she ran into me in the hall."

Beardall stared at him, plainly waiting on him to elaborate.

"What?"

Cole grinned. "Just because Bear looks like a Neanderthal doesn't mean he doesn't notice things."

"Brynnan's nice," said Bear.

"Yes," said Jack slowly. "She is, but—"

"But what?" Bear asked.

Jack glared at him. "Let's concentrate on keeping the security tight around here. If someone with deep pockets hired Nesser, the Austin shooter, and Fischer, they can hire replacements."

Cole grinned.

"What are you smiling about?" asked Jack.

"Hey, maybe we enjoy razzing you, but seriously, I've only been here a few hours and I can honestly say I've never seen you like this."

"Like what?" No, he shouldn't have asked that.

Cole looked more serious. "I've known you for ten years. You're really going to play this game? What's the matter anyway? Would Kade fire you if you asked her out?"

Bear linked his hairy arms across his chest. "Do it anyway."

"What?" Jack asked.

Bear spoke slowly, carefully enunciating his words. "Ask. Her. Out. Seriously dude, she's perfect for you."

"Bear, you just met her *today*."

"So?" answered Cole. "She's a sweet, funny, caring, Christian woman who's clearly more intelligent than you. And you're definitely into her. *Everyone* at dinner tonight could see that. If she's willing to put up with you, don't be an idiot."

Wow. He was really that transparent. Fantastic.

Jack rubbed the back of his neck. "Noted."

He knew how right they were. But that didn't

mean that it would work out. He had zero guarantee she'd like what she saw when she got to know him. When she knew everything.

"For now, let's focus on security. Start earning our paychecks. Bear, you take the first shift monitoring the cameras tonight from the security office. Cole, you relieve him at 0200."

"Roger that. What time will Max and TJ be here tomorrow?" Cole asked, referring to the two other men Jack hired.

"Late morning. I'll be gone, so you two show them around. We'll meet in the security office when I get back." Jack looked at his watch. "I need to check on something before it gets too late."

"Go on," said Beardall, "we can find our way back. We probably won't get lost. I brought a compass."

Jack shook his head. "See you later."

❦

Jack headed for the kitchen. The nagging thought hadn't waned. He realized it would be a constant distraction until he addressed it—and hopefully proved himself wrong.

Jack entered the kitchen, relieved Annalee was still around prepping for the next day's meals.

"Hi Annalee, sorry to bother you, but could I talk to you for a minute?"

"Oh, of course, of course," she said, setting a bowl of chopped peppers in the refrigerator. "What's on your mind?"

"It's about the man who died in the freezer a

couple of weeks ago."

"Oh," she said, covering her mouth with her hand. "That poor man. I feel so terrible."

Her voice hitched, and Jack felt awful. He didn't realize it was a sensitive topic.

"I'm sorry, I didn't mean to upset you, Annalee. I just wanted to understand what happened. If you'd rather me ask Mr. Kade my questions, I can."

"No, no. I can answer your questions. But I do feel guilty. This is my kitchen. I should have known the latch on the freezer was broken." She wrung her hands, her eyes moist.

Her tears made him feel like a jerk for bringing it up. Except...

She continued, "You see, I never close the door when I'm taking things in and out because I'm usually grabbing something real quick, and when we have a large delivery, I prop the door open."

"Wait a minute, you mean you didn't know the latch was broken?"

"No, I didn't. And it's my responsibility to make sure everything in the kitchen is properly maintained. I should have known it wasn't working. But believe me, I've been checking it every day since, and I'll continue doing that for the rest of my God-given days. Just imagine if Mr. Kade was having a big party and a child wandered in the freezer looking for ice cream and got locked in? Can you imagine? I still feel so terrible about that poor man."

Annalee's shoulders started to heave. Jack wrapped his arm around her.

"Annalee," he said gently, "I had no idea you felt this way, or I would have mentioned my suspicion to you sooner."

"What?" she asked confused.

"The only reason I asked you about what happened is because I wanted to see if Nesser could have been connected to it."

She still looked confused.

"Nick Nesser is the guy who broke into Brynnan's room last night."

"Oh, oh. Well, I don't see how he could have anything to do with it. The police showed me a picture of him early this morning when they were making their report. I told them I hadn't ever seen him before."

"I know, but just humor me for a minute. Mr. Kade said the man who died was found nearly twenty-four hours after being trapped in the freezer. Think about the day *before* you found him—the day he supposedly got accidentally trapped in the freezer. Who was on the premises *that* day? That was right after your last security guy left. I can't find any security footage from around that time."

"Yes, your predecessor, he was a whole different can of worms." She waved her hand in the air as if she could physically push that memory further away.

Jack was tempted to ask what she meant by that, but he didn't want to get sidetracked right now. He made a mental note to ask about that particular 'can of worms' later.

He turned around at a sound behind him.

"Hello," said Brynnan, entering the kitchen. "I was just going to make some hot tea." She paused, feeling she'd interrupted something. "Sorry, I didn't mean—"

"You're fine sweetheart, just fine," said

Annalee, wiping her eyes. "I can get that brewing for you. What kind would you like?" Annalee's genuine smile started to remerge.

Jack dropped his arm from her shoulders, still feeling guilty about upsetting her. He wanted to answer Brynnan's questioning expression, but only managed an awkward shrug.

"Don't go to any trouble. I'll make it myself," Brynnan offered. "Do you still have the peppermint tea I saw yesterday?"

"Oh, of course, dear, it's right here." Annalee fussed over Brynnan for a few minutes insisting on making the tea and suggesting all kinds of sweeteners for it.

"Sorry," she whispered to Jack while Annalee's top half was rooting around in a pantry. "I didn't mean to interrupt. Is she okay?"

"I think so."

He was afraid he knew the answer, but he couldn't keep himself from asking, "Any luck on the artifacts yet?"

She slumped into the chair next to him and rubbed her temples. "No. None." She accepted a cup of tea from Annalee. "Thank you so much, I needed a break."

"No problem at all, sweetheart. Do want something to eat?"

Brynnan smiled at the cheerful woman's incessant hospitality. "No, ma'am. The tea is wonderful. Thank you."

"Well, then, I'll just leave you two—"

Jack held up a hand. "No, please wait. I still want to ask you some things, if you don't mind." He turned to Brynnan. "I was asking Annalee about—"

He stopped himself, realizing Brynnan probably didn't know anything about the guy in the freezer. He quickly filled her in, not missing the suspicion in her eyes. She was on the same page he was.

"Ok, so that day, was there anyone here who was not a regular staff member, anyone I haven't met?"

Annalee furrowed her brow, giving the question her full concentration.

"Well, I've thought about that day a lot, naturally. And the police asked plenty of questions of everyone about that day. The only person who came to the ranch besides regular staff and that poor soul delivering plants, was our mailman."

"The mailman, that's all?"

"Yes. Mora tells me I'm supposed to say 'mail carrier' instead of 'mailman' but our 'mail carrier' is a *man*, so I think 'mailman' is okay. Don't you?"

"Yes, I'm sure it's fine. But you're certain he was the only one? And you saw him? It was your regular mailman that day?"

"Oh, yes, I remember that because Mr. Kade was mailing three packages to his brother that day. I kept them inside until I saw the mail truck pulling up because I was afraid it was going to rain that day and didn't want the packages to get wet. When he pulled up to the house, I went outside and asked him to come into the foyer to get the packages. He's such a sweet man—I knew he'd be happy to carry those boxes out for me. He was born and raised near here, in Navasota. I knew his Daddy—"

The look on Brynnan's face stopped Annalee mid-sentence. "What's wrong, sweetheart?"

"Oh, it's just, you said my uncle sent *three*

packages to my dad? That would be about a week before the accident?"

She exchanged a look with Jack. "The only packages my dad received from Marsten were the artifacts," she said. And her eyes told him, 'and there were only *two* packages.'

"Yes, I suppose that's what they were. Is everything okay?" asked Annalee.

"Oh, yes. I just remembered my dad said my uncle owned the museum his cousin was wanting to donate those items to. At the time I thought he was exaggerating." She shrugged with a shy smile. "I realize now he was probably right."

"He was," said Annalee. "The Brynton Museum."

Brynnan straightened, her eyes large. "I didn't even know that was the name of the museum. Brynton was my grandmother's maiden name, I'm named for her." Sadness crept into her still wide eyes. "It's…it's so strange learning so many things after my parents are gone. I didn't know there was a museum named after my grandmother, and I definitely didn't know Marsten had so much—" She felt Jack and Annalee's eyes on her and decided to stop herself. "Sorry. I didn't mean to get off-track."

"Don't you apologize about a thing," said Annalee. "You've been through an awful time." She patted Brynnan's shoulder.

"Back to the boxes," Jack said, looking at Annalee, "You're sure there were three?"

"Yes. I put all three boxes in the foyer myself that morning. I knew our mailman wouldn't be coming by until the afternoon, so I put them on the far side of the large planter near the door to keep them out of the way, but I know for sure I put three boxes there."

"And did you see the mailman pick up all three and carry them to his truck?"

"Well, no, I didn't stand there and watch him, I was on my way out to run over to the farmer's market for some okra. I told him where the packages were and thanked him and left. I know he took them all though because Mora cleaned the floor in the foyer later that afternoon and if there was a box laying around, she would have asked me about it, I'm sure of that."

"The mailman got there just as you were leaving? And that was while the plant delivery man was unloading?"

"Yes, he was still unloading when I left."

Jack noticed Brynnan looked uncomfortable, as if she wasn't sure she wanted to say something. He was certain Annalee had provided all the information she could, so he thanked her and added, "Please don't blame yourself about the freezer incident. I can't explain it all yet, but I think Nesser or someone he was working with may have had something to do with that broken latch."

"I don't know about that. It doesn't quite make sense to me, but I will say I'm glad you're here now. I think we're all much safer with you and your team looking after things."

"Thank you, ma'am. I promise to do my best."

"I know you will. I have a good feeling about you." He didn't want to consider the broad, conspiratorial, smile on her face. He was just relieved she was feeling better. He thanked her again and asked Brynnan if he could show her the extra cameras he had set up near her room. He knew that request would only encourage Annalee's train of thought and subsequent meddling, but he really needed to talk to Brynnan, privately.

❧

As they neared Brynnan's room, Jack pointed out cameras in the hallway and explained the cameras outside had a clear view of anyone approaching her windows but, reassured her no cameras were pointed *into* her windows.

"Thanks." She appreciated the explanation, but she was much more concerned about something else. "Could I talk to you for a second?"

"Sure."

He followed her into her room, shutting the door behind them. Too anxious to sit, she bypassed the sofa and stood near the fireplace.

"Brynnan, what's going on? Did you figure out something about the artifacts and not want to say it in front of Annalee? I could tell something was bothering you."

She shook her head. "No. No, unfortunately, I'm at a total loss on the artifacts so far. Which is the second thing I wanted to talk to you about."

"Okay, hang on, what was the first thing?" He smiled and sat on the sofa.

Oh, if he only knew what that smile did to me. She needed to stay focused. So much was happening. So much to worry about. She didn't need to keep noticing how incredibly attractive this man was.

She took a deep breath and reminded herself what had her so concerned. Her anxiety must have surfaced on her face because now Jack looked worried. "I started thinking about today. How did the guy with the knife—or whoever hired him—how did they know we were going to Mr. Krupp's house this afternoon? I hadn't told anyone exactly where I was going until you walked up while I was putting the box in my car."

Jack didn't look surprised. His face was almost…apologetic?

"I was going to tell you…"

"Tell me what?"

He stood, took a step toward her, his eyes serious. "You're right. It didn't make sense that someone was there waiting for us. It occurred to me too, I just didn't want to worry you until I was sure."

Now he *was* worrying her. "Sure of what exactly?"

She studied his eyes and sensed he was growing weary of voicing disturbing possibilities. His sensitivity to her feelings wrapped a warmth around her she had never experienced before. The confusion returned. Was he just the most compassionate head of security in the world, or was there something more to his motivation to protect her?

He steadied his gaze at her, and, though it pained him, he pushed forward with the truth. "When Fischer, the guy with the knife, made it clear it was the artifacts he wanted, it hit me. When Nesser tried to come up through the tunnel, he was trying to enter *your* room. How would he know where you kept the box, or what room you were in? And when we left for

Professor Krupp's house, I told no one exactly where we were going either. I only told Cole and Beardall I was going with you to drop something off at a friend's house. Someone knew the location of the box in the house, and where you were taking it today."

He prayed he wasn't scaring her, but he could see the anxiety on her face. He took a step closer to her, wanting to comfort her, wanting to hold her again.

She swallowed. "So…the house is *bugged*?"

He shook his head. "I thought about that, but no. I had Felix do a sweep. The house is clean."

She stared at him, unblinking. "Um…you 'had Felix do a sweep'…and 'the house is clean'?"

"Yeah."

She covered her face with her hands and whispered, "Unbelievable. I'm living in a Jason Bourne movie."

He didn't know how to respond to that.

She slid her hands from her face. Skepticism replacing her bewilderment. "So how *did* they know where we were going?"

"I think it's your phone. You said it was dead when we got back, so I knew you would be charging it and not using it this evening. That's why I hadn't mentioned it yet. I was going to ask you if I could borrow it after I talked to Annalee tonight."

He watched fear darken her face again. He couldn't stand that every other thing he'd said to her in the past twenty-four hours had caused that look.

"My phone? They bugged my phone?"

"We need to have Felix look at it to be sure, but yes, my gut says that's how they knew."

She grabbed her phone from where it was

charging on the dresser. "Ok, let's go. I want to know—"

Jack held up his hands. "Hang on, we have time. Felix stays up late, and I told him I'd come by later on to have him look at the phone. Now, what was the second thing you wanted to talk to me about?"

Brynnan's shoulders sagged. "The artifacts." She walked across the room, gesturing to the random vintage items spread across her king size bed. "Like I said, I'm at a total loss. I have no idea what's so exceptional about any of this."

He walked to her side and took in the collection. "So, you're going to have to help me here, what am I looking at? You said these were artifacts from early Texas. And none of it looks valuable?"

Brynnan shook her head, staring at the items—an iron, two Bowie knives, a Texas State Police badge, several arrowheads, four handkerchiefs, two buttons from some kind of uniform, two pewter mugs and a pair of women's shoes.

"Well, they'd be interesting additions to a Texas history museum. They're from several different decades, mainly eighteen hundreds. Though, the arrow heads could date back a thousand years. I'm not an expert on Native American history. It's possible none of these items are related to each other. They're most likely random items collected over the years. I can't give you an exact monetary value, but in general, unless someone could authenticate someone famous owned them or, that they were present at the Alamo or something, I don't see evidence of *exceptional* value. I mean, if one of the knives was used by Sam Houston or Davy Crockett, that would definitely make them more valuable, but I don't see how any of this is worth hiring mercenaries to retrieve."

Jack ran a hand through his hair and blew out a long breath. "The only thing that makes sense to me is that someone with plenty of money hired Nesser to steal one or several of these items. He grabs one box here, and maybe the plant delivery guy sees him, so he locks him in the freezer, and then he takes off before anyone else sees him. Then the other two boxes get mailed, so he has to drive to Austin to get them." He decided not to repeat the entire timeline that took place in Austin. "He's only able to take one of the boxes from the car, maybe he doesn't see the other one, or gets spooked by a witness to the wreck. Then, you bring the third box here, and he tries to get it while you're sleeping."

"But you said the house wasn't bugged. How would anyone know which room I was in that night? I didn't explain my location to anyone in a phone call."

"I know. But if they were listening to your phone, they were tracking it too. They would know which room your phone was in. Not much of a stretch that your phone would be in your room, with your things."

"Oh. Right. Wow. Like in the movies."

But this wasn't a movie. And it felt *really* creepy to be the one being spied on.

Brynnan took another long look at the artifacts and sighed. "I know you don't want to drive all over the state consulting experts on Texas history after what happened this afternoon, but if we want answers to the origins of these artifacts, it may come to that. Hopefully, Marsten's cousin can tell us something tomorrow, but if not, we're going to have to seek out some other historians. I'm pretty sure Professor Krupp won't feel like helping us now, but maybe the friend my parents were going to see, Dr. Drummond, could help. He's in Austin, but we could go later, if we don't get any answers tomorrow."

Jack nodded. "We could overnight the artifacts to him if we needed to, though I don't like the idea of them being out of our hands. And I wouldn't want to bring any danger to your parents' friend." He rubbed the scruff of his dark five o'clock shadow, that had showed up sometime after dinner. "If we decide we need his help, Cole and I can take the artifacts to him. It's safer if you stay here."

"No way. I'm not going to just sit here. Besides, Dr. Drummond knows me, it would be less awkward if I go with you. What happened today won't happen again, not if they only knew what we were doing because of my phone. They won't know where we're going this time. If it's safe for me to go tomorrow, to question Marsten's cousins, then it's safe for me to go to Austin."

"Honestly, Brynnan, you going tomorrow isn't the safest thing either."

She opened her mouth to protest, but he held up his hands. "I know we already decided you're going. I'm not changing that, but you have to understand, there's risk involved."

"I know. But they—whoever 'they' is—they only want the artifacts."

He admired her passion, and her courage, but she wasn't identifying all the threats. She wasn't trained to. He took another step forward, dangerously close to her personal space. "Brynnan, that's not true. Fischer made it very clear today, he wanted the artifacts *and* you. I think there's a reason for that. Either they think you know more about the artifacts than you do, or they want to use you to get something they need."

He watched her soak in his words for a few seconds. She was having to process so much. She was crazy smart, he'd learned that those first few days in Austin, but having to work through so many emotional pieces was difficult on a whole different level. He wanted to help. Not just help her put the pieces together—he wanted to be there for her when she saw the whole finished picture. Because it wasn't going to be pretty.

He knew he was standing too close to her, but he couldn't force himself to move away. He felt drawn to this woman like no one he'd ever known.

"I guess it's possible," she said, "that my parents weren't killed just because they had the artifacts, but because someone thought they *knew* their significance."

Jack watched her intently, praying this line of thinking didn't wreak havoc on her emotions again, not that he'd blame her. They didn't need to dwell on the what-ifs tonight though. "It's possible. But look, obviously, there's still plenty we don't know. Let's not start guessing right now. Let's take your phone to Felix, get some sleep, and hope we find out something from the cousins tomorrow."

Jack's phone buzzed. A text from his dad. It was an invitation to stop by the house, but the unusual wording he used told him more than the text itself.

"What's wrong?" asked Brynnan.

"It's from my dad. He wants to talk. And not on the phone. He wants me to come by the house."

"You look like you think it's bad news. I know what you said about not completely ruling anything out, but I thought it was looking like this didn't have anything to do with the Alesi family, or their enemies."

"I know. I don't know exactly what he wants to talk about, but I can tell it's work related. I need to check in with him."

Her eyes grew distant, her thoughts seeming a million miles away. He stood there for a couple of beats. "Brynnan?"

He watched her pull her gaze back to his, as if it was difficult. "What's wrong?"

"He may have read my file."

"Maybe, but like I said, no one is trying to invade your privacy, everyone is just trying to keep you and your uncle safe."

"I know. I know it's your job. But...you might...you won't like what's in there."

Then it hit him like a wall of bricks—she didn't want *him* to know details about the times she was held captive. She cared what *he* thought. His gut twisted.

Something in her eyes—something he couldn't articulate—knocked the breath out of him.

"Brynnan… I'm not trying to dig up your past. I'm trying to protect you."

"I understand. You're just doing your job. It's okay."

Second time she'd said that.

Did she really not know? What he was really

saying...the truth behind his words.

She needed to understand.

He took a chance, cupped her face in his hands and ran his thumb down her cheek. "I'd do anything to make all this easier on you—I'd do anything to make it all go away."

She pressed his hands against her face, savoring his touch and everything behind it—knowing what was behind it, not denying the possibility anymore.

She felt the tears forming. She saw the way he looked at her. She understood it. But as much as she wanted to explore everything that might be between them, she knew as soon as he knew everything, everything she'd done, that look would vanish.

She tamped down the emotion, refused the tears.

She needed to tell him everything, get this over with. It baffled her that they'd grown so close in a little over a week but, suddenly, denying it felt ridiculous. Now, the longer she waited to show him who she really was, the more painful it would be when he turned away. Which he would.

"Jack, I need to explain. You don't know me as well as you think you do." She squeezed his hands and lowered them from her face. She needed some space. If she was going to explain this, she couldn't do it feeling his touch.

She walked to the sofa, falling onto the seat with her head in her hands. She sensed him sit beside her. Thankfully, he kept some distance between them.

Lord, please give me the strength...the words. Make him see... Protect him from my past. And present.

A tendril of peace curled around her heart. A fortifying breath later, she began her story.

"The first time I was taken, I was sixteen. The guy was…cruel. He said so many terrible things to me…hit me."

Then again, maybe Jack didn't need the play-by-play. Some things, she needed to say though.

"But, he never…" she looked at him hoping he hadn't assumed the creep had tried to… "It was physical and verbal abuse, but he didn't…it could have been much worse. I was always grateful for that."

This would probably be easier if she stared at the floor or something while she talked. But she couldn't pull her eyes from Jack's gaze. He was emanating so much compassion, it nearly undid her.

"Anyway, he totally terrified me. I didn't have any faith then. I didn't know God. I felt so alone and helpless. I just caved. I had zero strength. I was completely pitiful. When the FBI showed up, I was just a crying mess." She took another deep breath and allowed herself one more moment to relish in his gaze, before that light was doused permanently.

"Over time, everything I experienced turned to anger. I was never going to let that happen to me again. If I was ever in danger again, I was going to fight with everything I had…and that's exactly what I did." She knew he could see the pain building in her eyes. He already looked hurt and she hadn't even explained. *Just get this over with.*

"When I was taken again two years later, I was still plenty scared, but I wasn't going to give up. Not like the first time."

"You were stronger."

She shook her head. "No!" she said, louder

than she'd intended. "It wasn't strength, it was just anger and hate. I still didn't know God at that time. I wasn't leaning on Him for mental strength to make it through, or physical strength to defend myself. I just…" she broke down. Emotion threatening to suffocate her. She couldn't finish. She'd hadn't spoken any of this out loud in years. It was so much more difficult than she thought it would be. Fine. At least Jack was seeing the truth. He'd see why he needed to stop looking at her the way he had been.

Jack reached for her, but she pushed him away.

She stood and backed away from him, trying to maintain some composure. She steeled herself and continued. "They…there were three of them, three men the second time. And they weren't any nicer than the first guy. They told me over and over that they were going to kill me. They were waiting for Bobby Alesi, my grandfather, they wanted him to watch—to exact some gruesome revenge on him."

She sighed. This was exhausting. She was glad he didn't try to interrupt again, that would just make it more difficult.

She wiped her face and continued. "I was with them for three days. They gave me a bathroom break every few hours. It became routine. They didn't see me as any kind of threat, just an eighteen-year-old girl. They didn't know what was going on in my mind, my level of determination. One of them finally got careless. He left his gun on the kitchen counter. It was still sitting there when they let me walk to the bathroom."

Silence hung in the air for several long seconds before she finally said, "I killed them. All three of them. I murdered them. Don't you see? That's what I meant when I said I'm not the person you think I am. I'm a…I'm a…"

"No, you're not." Jack sprang from the sofa, but she took another step back, feeling undeserving of the consolation she sensed coming.

"Brynnan, that was *self-defense*, not murder."

"That's what the FBI said. There were no charges filed. They said those guys had no intention of letting me live. They said if I hadn't shot them, I'd be dead."

"Then that was the truth. The FBI agents wouldn't have said that just to make you feel better. If that's what they told you, then they were certain of it."

She shook her head again, looking no less tortured than moments ago. "You don't understand. It's not the fact that I took their lives—I know self-defense isn't a sin—but it's *why* I did it that's so horrible. I wasn't thinking about escape when I pulled the trigger. I was consumed with so much hatred— from *both* kidnappings. That night, I wasn't defending myself, I was exacting revenge."

That was it. She'd finally gotten out everything she'd wanted to say. Emotion roiled inside her. Tried to swallow her. Her knees buckled. She wobbled.

Jack lunged forward. His strong arms wrapped around her, steadying her, holding her up until she looked him in the eyes.

When she was standing firmly on her own, he placed his hands on her shoulders, willing her to understand everything he wanted to say.

"Brynnan, you can't beat yourself up like this. I know you're a strong woman of faith now. Anyone can see that. God has forgiven you. And like you said, you weren't even a believer at the time. God erased *all* your sin when you came to Him. 'If anyone is in Christ, the new creation has come: the old is gone, the new is here.' Your slate's clean as far as God's concerned."

"I know. I know who I am as a child of God. But that's not how people see things. People are human. And when they learn what I did..."

He ran his hands up and down her arms. Emotion constricted his throat. Emotion he promised himself he'd never allow again. But a new version of those feelings definitely woke something inside him. And in a more profound way than ever before.

"I can't speak for others, Brynnan, but I want you to know I *don't* think less of you. The Brynnan I know is the new Brynnan. That's all that matters. I don't care what you did before."

She looked stunned. "But how can you see past..."

He smiled and ran his thumb down her cheek again. "I can't say I haven't struggled with similar things. Like I told you, I was an Army Ranger, for twelve years. And we didn't deploy all over the world to help little old ladies cross the street. I've seen the kind of evil you saw in those men. I've seen it over and over again. I've watched innocent men, women and children die at the hands of that kind of evil. So, yeah, I've struggled, at times, with making sure I carried out my duties with the right mindset. The difference is, I was a believer before I joined the Army. I don't want to think about how I would have handled certain situations if I hadn't known God."

He couldn't believe he was standing here saying all this. To *this* woman. He'd never said some of these things out loud, ever. To *anyone*. *What was he doing?* He felt more vulnerable than he ever had in his life. But taking in her face, at that moment, reading everything there, he knew he wasn't finished.

"I've taken lives, Brynnan. I didn't enjoy it. But sometimes evil gives you no other alternative. And I just have to trust God to guide me through those situations."

He watched unshed tears well in her eyes and wondered if he'd made a mistake, said too much. He didn't normally talk about himself this much. Scratch that—he had *never* talked about himself this much. And there were still things she didn't know. But maybe now wasn't the time. He wasn't sure what she was thinking. He wasn't completely sure she was breathing.

"Brynnan, what matters right now is that you believe your past doesn't change the way I see you at all. If anything, I admire you more for sharing that with me. I know it wasn't easy."

Her bright, beautiful eyes stared at him in near disbelief.

Her lip quivered. And he nearly lost it. He pulled her to him and held her tight against his chest. He cradled her head with one arm and rubbed her back with the other. She sobbed into his shirt until he could feel her tears on his skin. Relief that she was allowing him to comfort her washed over him. He rested his chin on the top of her head.

He was in deep. So deep.

After a minute, she eased back. "Sorry about

your shirt."

His phone buzzed. He didn't move.

"Go ahead. Answer it," she said through a teary smile.

He pulled his cell out and answered the call. "McKerrick...Yes, we'll be there shortly. But first, do a sweep on all of Mr. Kade's vehicles. ...Okay, thanks. We'll meet you in fifteen." He ended the call and watched Brynnan's eyebrows raise.

"The cars?"

"Yeah." He pushed a hand through his hair, frustration clouding his eyes. "That was Felix. I just remembered, when he called, that I had him check the house but not the cars. I'll have him check the house, cars, and our phones regularly until all this is settled."

His comments jerked her back to all the problems around them. She didn't want to wrestle with all that just yet. She was enjoying a new freedom she hadn't felt before. The man she'd confided in years ago may have looked at her like she was a criminal, but the man standing in front of her right now never would. Somehow, she *knew* that.

She'd been telling herself for years that she trusted God. And she did—to an extent. But days ago, when she felt God telling her she could trust Jack, she'd balked. Now she realized there was no way a man like Jack could be in her life unless God put him there.

She wanted to say something. Something profound. But all she could muster was, "Thank you."

"For checking for bugs?"

"Well, yes, but more so for everything else.

For everything you said. You have no idea what it means to me."

He looked at her with a tenderness she'd never seen in him before. Slowly, his hands slid over her cheeks and into her hair. Heat shot through her as she watched his eyes roam her face, searching, longing, asking. He leaned down, hovering an inch away, his breath teasing her lips. She held still, suddenly aware of how desperately she wanted him to close the distance. And he did.

His lips were soft and, incredibly tender. She wrapped her arms around his neck, and his kiss grew stronger. She reciprocated with a soft groan, holding tight, blissfully drowning in him. And for a few moments, everything else in the world disappeared.

Completely consumed in his kiss, she forgot about crime families, spooky tunnels, shooters and artifacts.

Until his phone buzzed, again.

They ignored the disruption for a few seconds.

Then, reluctantly, he ended the kiss and, sliding his hands to her face, rested his forehead on hers. They heard the call go to voicemail.

Jack eased back and looked into her eyes. His Adam's apple bobbed. "I didn't plan that," he whispered, his voice thick, husky, and a little out of breath. "I didn't mean to overstep...I don't want to take advantage..."

"I appreciate that." She smiled. "But I could have stopped you." Her smile broadened. "I did *not* want to stop you."

Before he knew what he was doing, he returned his lips to hers, with a fervor pulsating through him unlike anything he'd ever felt before. She felt perfect in his arms. And her kiss was undoing him.

Until his phone interrupted. *Again.*

Brynnan smiled against his lips and failed at stifling her laugh. "I think you're going to have to answer it."

Jack took out his phone, wanting to strangle whoever was on the other end of the call.

It was Felix again. He answered the call on speaker.

"I found something."

Now he had Jack's full attention. "In the cars? Are they bugged?"

"Just Brynnan's. Not a listening device. Just a tracker. Still, thought you'd want to know."

"Yes. Thanks, Felix. We're on our way to you now."

The meeting with Felix was quick. Jack kept the exchange as short as possible when he realized how excited Felix was to see Brynnan.

"Leave the tracker on Brynnan's car. They don't know we know about it. We may want to use that to our advantage later. Get her phone checked out. I need to head out on an errand, but text me as soon as you know something."

"Sure," said Felix. He apparently didn't think it odd for anyone to be running an errand at ten o'clock at night. Jack figured Felix was the type to stay up at all hours.

Felix turned his attention to Brynnan. "Are you going too? The phone will just take a minute, if you want to stay..."

"If it won't take long, yes. I want to know for sure if anyone has been listening to my calls."

Jack could read Felix, and his overconfidence, too plainly. He was *not* comfortable with Brynnan staying in Felix's office, but he couldn't think of a rational sounding reason to suggest she leave. He was afraid if he opened his mouth, he'd sound overprotective. Or jealous.

Brynnan looked amused. Was she reading his mind?

"I'll be fine," she assured him.

Fine. It was getting late. He really needed to check in with his dad. He went ahead and threw a threatening glare at Felix on his way out. Hopefully, the flirtatious tech took the hint.

Twenty-five minutes later he was pulling into his parents' driveway. This wasn't the type of visit he'd imagined himself making when he decided to work for Marsten Kade, but it was a nice change to be such a short drive from family for once.

His mom opened the front door as soon as he stepped on the porch. "Hey sweetheart, come on in." She hugged him and kissed his cheek. "I know you're here on business, but are you hungry? Want something to drink? I made up some peach tea today, want some?"

"Yes, thanks. Sorry to stop by so late. It's been a long day."

Her eyes turned serious. "I know. Your dad gave me the highlights. And he told me about what happened in Austin." She sighed, familiar worry in her eyes. "I know Mr. Kade is very lucky to have you, but honestly, I didn't think this job would be so dangerous."

"I didn't either. But at least it's not boring." He smiled, trying to lighten her concern.

She shook her head and shooed him down the hall. "I'll bring you some tea. Your dad is in the study."

He entered his dad's large study to find papers and photographs spread out all across the long table that sat perpendicular to his desk. The table had once been his grandmother's dining table, but for as long as he could remember, it occupied nearly half his dad's study, usually covered with files. Tonight, the files pertained to Brynnan. Her family. Her past. This meeting already felt surreal.

His dad smiled when Jack walked in. He shook his son's hand and pulled him into a hug. "Well, it's not the best of circumstances, but I'm glad to see you. After the week or so you've had, I'm glad to see you in one piece."

"Thanks. I hope I didn't put you in an awkward position requesting information. But it didn't make sense for me not to at least ask. What do you think about all this? Your message sounded like you knew something."

"I do. I'll tell you what I've been told, unofficially, but you're going to have a lot of questions I don't have answers to."

"I understand."

Jack's mom appeared with peach tea and snickerdoodle cookies. When she left, Jack slid into one of his dad's leather armchairs and waited for him to continue.

"First of all, I got a quick response from a friend of mine about your text earlier tonight. A few years ago, your tunnel intruder, Nesser, briefly shared a cell with the delivery guy who died in Mr. Kade's freezer."

"Why am I not surprised?" Jack leaned back in his chair processing that information.

"I don't think it looks like the delivery guy was in on Nesser's plan."

"I agree. I'm thinking Nesser snuck onto the property, possibly using the tunnels, to steal the boxes Marsten was mailing to Brynnan's parents. His old cell mate just happens to be making a delivery at the same time and recognizes him."

"And Nesser kills him to cover his tracks."

"Yep. Which took longer, and messed with his window of opportunity, because he only got away with one box instead of all three." He leaned forward, his elbows on his knees, and sighed. "Then he tracked the other two boxes to Austin and killed Brynnan's parents trying to get them." He looked at his dad. "I know some of it is conjecture, but these boxes are leaving a trail of bodies and violence."

His dad leaned against his desk, his expression grim. "And Brynnan was in possession of the last box when the shooter showed up in Austin, when Nesser showed up under her room, *and* today, when y'all were attacked at the professor's house. Sounds like Miss Brynnan Marsh is lucky to be alive. And I believe she has you to thank for that."

Jack shook his head. "She's had three *close calls* while under my protection. I'm not proud of that. I need to start anticipating these guys."

"Well, I'd start by making sure Brynnan is nowhere near that box."

"I know. It's not in her room. I locked it in a

safe in the security office at the ranch before I left to come here tonight. But," he rubbed his temples, cringing at what he was about to voice, "I'm concerned they may target Brynnan with or without the box."

"Why?"

"Because maybe she's the only one who's looked at the artifacts with enough expertise to actually figure out whatever they're trying to hide. I'm not convinced Nesser was forced to kill Brynnan's parents just to acquire the box and cover his tracks."

"You think he killed them to silence any discovery they'd made or would eventually make?"

"Unfortunately, I have to consider it a possibility."

"Does Brynnan realize all this? And how much danger she's in?"

Jack's gut twisted. He hoped his dad couldn't read how much pain her fear was causing him. "Yes, she does." He sighed and changed the subject. "Did you hear anything else from any of your contacts?"

"Some. The FBI is reasonably sure the shooter in Austin, Nesser, and your knife attacker were all hired by the same person, but all I've been told is that the guy is in Houston. To be honest, I don't think anyone is sure of much more than that. There are theories no one is willing to share yet. I got the impression this is overlapping into some ongoing investigations, so there's only so much anyone can discuss."

Jack started to comment, but his dad held up a finger.

"The other piece of information is that the guy with the knife and the shooter in Austin, at one time, worked for Paul Casper."

"Let me guess, he's involved in organized crime on the west coast?"

"Yes. And before you ask, he's no friend of Bobby Alesi. I don't know about a current feud, but they're not friendly. However, these two men apparently haven't worked for Casper in a while. No one I talked to thinks Casper has anything to do with this mastermind in Houston."

"But that's too much of a coincidence. *Two* of Casper's men come after Brynnan and her parents? It has to be connected to Casper somehow."

"Does the Houston connection make sense to you?" asked his dad.

"Well, Marsten is suspicious of his cousins. Three of them live in Houston. I don't know of any connection between his cousins and Alesi, but his cousin, Victor, is the one who sent Marsten the boxes of artifacts in the first place, so I'd love to get that figured out. Marsten seems very suspicious of all his cousins, which is unsettling. Frankly, at the moment, I don't know where else to look. We're going to Houston tomorrow to talk to them. Marsten thinks we'll learn a lot more in person."

Jack related the conversations he and Brynnan had with Marsten that afternoon.

"Hold on," his dad looked concerned, "why are you taking Brynnan with you tomorrow? That sounds like an unnecessary risk."

Jack shut his eyes and pinched the bridge of his nose. "I know," he finally said. "It's stressing me out, to be honest. It's not safe. But she *really* wants to go. And Marsten doesn't want to tell her she can't come."

Yeah, I'll just blame that on Marsten, because I'm so sure I could tell her no.

"I understand he's your boss, but as his head of security, couldn't you stress how dangerous this could be in front of both of them to try to persuade her not to go?"

Um, yeah, but then I would be telling her no.

Jack didn't answer right away. He felt his dad studying him. "It wouldn't do any good. I've explained the risks. We're just going to have to be careful." He glanced at the files on the dining table. He noticed Marsten's name. "You have anything here that would be helpful?"

"Just background information on Marsten Kade, and Brynnan." He paused. "How much do you know about what happened to her when she was a teenager?" He gestured to several pictures Jack hadn't focused on yet.

When he saw the images, bile rose in his throat. Brynnan. As a teenager. Bruised and bloody.

He'd seen worse in person, witnessed horrible atrocities while deployed overseas, but...but this was Brynnan. He'd known the facts beforehand, but he hadn't prepared himself to see the pictures. As if he could have.

He noticed his dad studying him again. "Yes, I know about the kidnappings. Is there anything else in these files that links our recent attackers to Alesi?"

"No, not that I've found. I will give you a heads up about Mr. Kade's family though. The FBI doesn't have any evidence of Marsten's involvement in anything illegal, but he may be the only Kade who isn't under some level of scrutiny from the FBI or local law enforcement. I don't know specifics but, be careful tomorrow. I'm told the family tree is pretty twisted."

"That tracks with how Marsten describes them. Tomorrow should be interesting." Jack shoved all the pictures into a folder. He felt better with them out of sight.

"So, tell me about Brynnan," his dad said, sitting on the edge of his desk and crossing his arms across his chest. "What's she like?"

"She's strong. She's handling all this as well as can be expected. Her faith is well grounded. That was a huge relief. I can't imagine how hard all this would be for her otherwise. She's crazy smart—"

His dad was looking at him with an expression he didn't understand. "What?"

"You didn't tell me you cared about her."

Great.

He should've expected this. If Cole and Bear could read him, his FBI father could.

He was sure his face was confirming all his dad's suspicions.

"Look, right now I'm just trying to concentrate on keeping her safe. When all this is over, if there's anything to tell, I'll update you."

"Fair enough." His dad smiled.

Jack finished the last of his tea. "I need to get back. Thanks for the information."

Deep concern creased his father's face. "Jack, be careful tomorrow. I think you have your work cut out for you with the Kade family."

"That may be an understatement." He grabbed a few cookies for the road. "Thanks, again. I'll be in touch."

Jack walked back to his truck with a growing

uneasiness that his dad's concern about the eccentric Kade family was well placed. He planned on keeping his guard up around Marsten's cousins the next day.

CHAPTER EIGHT

The next morning found Brynnan wide awake long before her alarm chimed, anxious about the day ahead and what it may hold. She tried not to focus on how surreal it all was—what they were doing and why they were doing it. She even changed her clothes four times, which she knew was ridiculous, but really, what does one wear to question billionaires about their possible involvement in murder?

Especially alongside Jack. The memory of his kiss the night before flooded her thoughts—a million 'what-ifs' swirling through her mind. Jack McKerrick felt so *real*—not just his kiss, but *him* in her life. The notion was blissful. And terrifying. What if she was wrong about him? What if she wasn't?

She finally cleared her mind enough to decide on a pair of navy linen pants, a pink blouse and sandals, and forced herself out the door before she doubted her choice for the fourth time.

On her way to meet up with Jack and her

uncle, she prayed for answers to so many questions. About her parents, the artifacts, the attacks, whether her life was in danger, the Alesis. And Jack.

It's all in your sovereign hands, God. Please give me wisdom to navigate the unknown, for I know it's only unknown to me, You know all things. And please keep us all safe. Amen.

Lifting off the helipad, situated just beyond Annalee's vegetable garden, Jack and Brynnan both acted as best they could as if they were accustomed to flying from one billionaire's estate to another's via private helicopter.

They headed to the historic River Oaks area of Houston, home to many of Houston's oldest oak trees and most affluent citizens—two Kade cousins in particular.

Their first stop was the eldest of the Kade cousins, Victor. When they landed at Victor Kade's nineteen thirties, English Tudor style home, they were promptly met at the edge of the helipad by whichever staff member whose job it was to greet visitors at the helipad. This young man ushered them inside where a more senior, and apparently superior, staff member, greeted them. He was a silver haired gentleman who fit the part of old English butler so perfectly he could have walked right out of a nineteenth-century British novel.

Jack struggled to keep a straight face. If his name was Jeeves, he was going to lose it.

"Good morning Mr. Kade," the silver haired gentlemen greeted them with a ridiculous air of formality, as if they were about to meet the Queen of England. "Mr. Kade will receive you in the courtyard."

"Thank you, Darlington. This is my niece, Brynnan Marsh and my head of security, Jack McKerrick."

Darlington gave a short nod. "This way," he instructed, leading them through a cavernous hallway. "I will announce you."

His name wasn't Jeeves. But 'Darlington' was bad enough. Jack doubted Beardall or Cole could've kept their composure at the receiving end of Darlington's judgmental glare. It was a good thing they'd stayed back at the ranch. This butler, or manservant, or whatever role he performed, was overplaying his part. Jack tried not to roll his eyes.

Marsten followed Darlington, leaving Brynnan and Jack to fall in step behind them. Jack leaned into Brynnan's ear. "We're going to be announced," he whispered.

Brynnan rolled her lips in and bit down to keep from laughing. She kept her eyes forward, but he enjoyed the grin she couldn't suppress.

"Sir," Darlington's deep, efficient voice broadcasted the trio's arrival to the courtyard. "Mr. Kade, Miss Marsh and Mr. McKerrick."

Victor Kade was standing poolside, barefoot, in a bright Hawaiian shirt with not-so-natural-looking tanned skin and peroxide blond hair. He was holding some kind of bag.

"Ah, thank you Darlington," he called out, without leaving the pool area.

Darlington gave his signature short nod and left.

"Come, come," said Victor, motioning his guests toward the pool. He grinned and gestured broadly at the water. "Aren't they magnificent?"

Everyone looked into the pool. Jack was not prepared for what he saw. They had walked right out of nineteenth century England into a scene from a James Bond movie.

Sharks. Victor Kade was actually standing by a pool of sharks, chumming the water no less. Jack took in Victor's appearance, his weird smile, the bloody meat, and sharks. Yep, he was pretty sure Victor was going for 'Bond villain.' Which was disturbing on so many levels.

Marsten didn't seem surprised or impressed. "Yes, you have some interesting pets."

Jack noted his boss's patronizing tone was thinly veiled. Maybe he should have inquired more about Marsten's relationship with his cousin before this meeting.

"That they are," agreed Victor, as if Marsten's comment had been completely genuine.

"Victor, I don't believe you've met my niece, Brynnan."

"Oh yes, a pleasure to meet you. I was sorry to hear about your parents. My condolences."

"Thank you," she answered, but he'd already returned his attention to his sharks who were circling nearby in anticipation of more meat.

Marsten glared at the back of his cousin's head. "Victor, we're pressed for time today. Could we pull you away from your fish for a moment?"

"They're sharks, Marsten. They're actually...oh never mind. You said on the phone you had some questions about security. I don't see how I could help you with that." He looked at Jack. "And *my* security is top notch."

Jack knew that was supposed to be a jab but didn't say a word.

Marsten decided to get right to it. "Victor, the night before last, someone tried to break into my house. They accessed space underneath the house by way of those tunnels you and I and the other cousins explored when we were kids."

Jack watched Victor's face closely.

Victor's eyes narrowed. "Well, you're the one who wanted to get out of Houston and move out to the sticks." He threw another handful of meat into the pool. The bloody splashing and thrashing that followed clearly entertained Victor.

Brynnan took a step back. More because of Victor's creepy smile than the sharks. But also, the sharks.

Jack sensed growing tension between the two Kade cousins and decided to intervene with his own questions. "Sir, we were hoping you could help us figure out who might have knowledge of the tunnels. It's very unlikely the intruder came across the hidden entrance he used by accident. Can you think of any way he may have heard about the tunnels?"

"Well, they've never been a secret." He looked at Marsten. "It's not like we were told not to tell anyone about them."

"Actually, as kids, I think we were specifically told that. I still have no idea as to their original purpose, but I do remember being told not to advertise their existence. Why would the family want the world to know there was a tunnel system under the country property? Aunt Agnes lived out there for thirty years. You know she didn't want anyone traipsing around undetected."

"They told us all kinds of balderdash when we were kids." He set down the bag of meat on a patio chair, held up his hand, and ticked off his list with his fingers. "The tunnels are haunted, the tunnels are full of snakes, the tunnels were dug out by a clan of Sasquatches, the tunnels were a hideout for bank robbers, and Great-uncle Arthur ran a brewery down there during prohibition." He stopped and stared at his hand as if the list was actually written there. "Come to think of it, besides the ghosts and the Sasquatches, the rest might have been true. In any case, I've disregarded anything that was ever told to me about those tunnels. Sure, I've told people about them. What does it matter? Do the police really need your help in trying to find your intruder?"

Victor directed his statements at Marsten, but Jack decided he should answer. "The police already arrested the intruder." He exchanged glances with Marsten before proceeding. "We learned he has a lawyer. Mitch Kandle. I understand you are familiar with him."

"Yes, of course I am. So is your boss." He nodded to Marsten.

"Yes," said Marsten, "but I've never hired him."

"Is that what this is about? You think because Kandle has worked for me in the past that I know what's going on? I don't keep tabs on Kandle."

"No, Mr. Kade," said Jack. "We suspect the intruder was *hired* to break into your cousin's home the other night and we are trying to figure out who might have hired him and why. Are you familiar with any of Mr. Kandle's other clients?"

Victor balled his fists and flushed with anger,

but the blood rising in his face mixed with his unnatural tan turned his expression a sickening shade of orange. "You suspect me, don't you? You're crazy!" His eyes shot daggers at Marsten with so much hatred Jack was sure the present conversation wasn't the only issue striking discord between the cousins.

"Victor," Marsten's voice was even, "we did not come to accuse you, we came to see if you could shed any light on the subject."

"Like what? I didn't hire Kandle for that man, and I don't know who did!"

"Well perhaps you could indulge us with some other information?" Marsten said, nodding to Jack a second time.

Jack took his cue. "We also have a suspicion that the man who broke in may have intended to steal some of the items you sent to your cousin as a donation to his museum. Do you have any idea which of those items may have been worth such a risk?"

"That old stuff? You think that's what he wanted? You *are* crazy."

The hairs on Jack's neck stood rigid. Victor was lying. He was sure of it. Victor wasn't a terrible liar, but he wasn't very good either. Jack decided to press. "Mr. Kade, the same man is suspected of causing the accident that took the lives of Brynnan's parents—"

"Whoa! What? And you think I hired him? I never… Are you accusing me of murder now?" His volume was all the way up.

Brynnan observed silently until that point. Listening to her parents' deaths being discussed was surreal, but the conversation with Victor was quickly derailing, and she *needed* to glean something helpful from this trip. The men didn't seem to be diffusing the situation any time soon, so she decided to take a different approach with Victor Kade.

"Mr. Kade," she said, employing her sweetest, most innocent tone, "There's one thing I just can't figure out. It seems whoever caused my parents' accident also stole one of the boxes you sent for Uncle Marsten's museum. I looked through some of the artifacts, and I just have no idea what could be of such importance. Do you remember if anything was of more value than the other objects?" Her words were all sugar and spice and everything nice. With a measured amount of dumb blond purposefully mixed in.

Jack was impressed. Her act was well played. And it was working on Victor.

Victor's expression softened. He smiled, too much, at Brynnan. "Oh, my dear, again I'm very sorry about your parents. I'm afraid I wasn't very familiar with the items I sent to Marsten. I found them stored in a boat I recently purchased from my cousin, Hershel. He collects antique bits of this and that. Historical artifacts are far outside my areas of expertise, but I was sure Marsten could put them to good use in his museum."

"Oh, I see," she said. Brynnan had more questions now. But she thought it best to pose them to her uncle after they left Victor's house.

"You purchased the boat from Hershel?" asked Marsten.

"Yes," said Victor, without taking his eyes off Brynnan.

Marsten kept his tone civil, just short of patronizing. "Thank you for your help, Victor. It sounds like we need to ask Hershel about the contents of the boxes. Sorry to have bothered you today. Could your driver take us to Hershel's? I'd like to speak with him about all this."

Victor turned to Marsten and rolled his eyes, then broke into a grin. "You're right about one thing, cousin, he won't talk to you on the phone. Best to just show up. Will you be accusing him of nefarious deeds as well?"

Marsten ignored the comment. "Thank you for your hospitality," said Marsten, without attempting to sound sincere.

Victor rolled his eyes again. "Darlington can show you out," he said, and the butler materialized before them. "I'll have my driver meet you out front. Say hi to Hershel for me." His attention shifted back to Brynnan. "Sweetheart, you really don't need to go with them, do you? You could wait here with me. We'll have a lovely lunch here in the courtyard. You can feed the sharks with me."

"That's so kind of you, but I really should go too," she said.

"Nonsense! I'm sure my cousin and his head of security can find out if Hershel knows anything about this unfortunate business. They'll have to come back later for the helicopter anyway. You and I can enjoy lunch, I'll open a bottle of wine—"

"She said no," said Jack. He did not raise his voice, but the firmness in his words caused Victor to recoil. Victor had lied several times that morning, but he wasn't lying about wanting Brynnan to stay behind with him. Not. Happening.

183

Brynnan looked at Jack, but he didn't meet her eyes. Part of her wanted to say, 'I can say 'no' all by myself,' but this Victor guy was seriously disturbed. She was a little relieved Jack intimidated him. She could definitely say 'no', and do more than that if she had to, but she had an uncomfortable feeling that Victor Kade might possibly be more than she could handle by herself, if she was alone. She made a mental note to be sure that never happened.

"Thank you anyway," said Brynnan politely. "But we really should be going." She led the trio to the far end of the courtyard where Darlington was waiting for them. They heard the thrashing and splashing resume as they walked out.

Darlington paraded them back through the long hallway and, without a word, deposited them in the care of Victor's driver. Moments later they were on their way to Hershel Kade's home.

Marsten looked back at the house, momentarily lost in thought. "I know we could have asked those questions of Victor over the phone, but I wanted to see his face."

"You don't trust him," said Jack.

"No, I don't," said Marsten.

"I'm glad to hear that. Because he was lying."

Marsten raised his eyebrows, surprised at the finality of Jack's assertion. Then a hint of a grin crept into his expression. "I knew you were a man of many talents. I agree with you completely. He knows something."

Brynnan looked worried. "I guess that gives us some clue, I mean, I guess we're looking in the right direction, but we still don't have any proof. We can't go to the police and say Victor looked like he was lying. And if Victor did hire Nesser, we still don't know *why*."

Jack nodded. "There's more to it. He *had* the boxes in his possession, then mails them to your uncle. *Then* hires a mercenary to steal them back at all costs? We definitely don't have the whole picture. I'm just convinced Victor is guilty of *something*."

"Maybe Hershel can shed some light on all this," said Marsten.

"Anything we should know about Hershel before we get there?" asked Jack as the car meandered through the stately River Oaks neighborhood.

Marsten sighed. "He's smarter than Victor. And not quite as eccentric. No pet sharks."

Jack was hoping Marsten had a better relationship with Hershel than Victor. He was positive Marsten and Victor's strained relationship stemmed from some kind of epic family feud. But his boss wasn't divulging anything. Jack decided if it seemed relevant to their current concern, he would ask Marsten about it when they got back to the ranch, but he knew it was probably a sibling quarrel with no connection to Nesser.

Brynnan seemed to be on the same train of thought. "Why did he say your other cousin, Hershel, wouldn't talk to you on the phone?" she asked.

Her uncle sighed, but his eyes smiled. "You have to understand Hershel. He only talks to people when he wants to talk to them. If he doesn't call you, he doesn't want to talk to you. If you call and leave a message, he pretends he didn't get it. I believe the kids now call that 'ghosting.' It's not new. People have been ignoring people they don't want to talk to for ages. The millennials just gave it a name."

Brynnan smiled. "I see." She looked thoughtful for a moment. "If you don't mind me saying, I noticed you and Victor don't seem to get along very well."

Jack was surprised at her bluntness. And eager to hear his boss's response.

"No, we don't." He didn't seem at all bothered by her observation but declined to offer any explanation.

"Well, I just mention it because I thought it seemed odd that he wanted to donate the boxes of artifacts to your museum. He doesn't seem interested in the artifacts at all, and the two of you don't get along so well…"

"Ah, yes. That's easy to explain. Victor knows all donors of artifacts have to meet with the head of acquisitions for the museum, Darla Upton." He paused, seeming to search for his words. "Miss Upton is very attractive. She's too young for him, I think, but he doesn't care what I think. Victor has tried more than once to cross paths with her, but to no avail. So, when he found 'some old stuff' as he calls it, he immediately wanted to donate it to the museum and set an appointment with Miss Upton. That's why I wanted your dad to verify the contents of the boxes first. I didn't want to bother Darla with them if it was just a pathetic attempt by Victor to talk to a pretty girl."

Jack couldn't believe what he was hearing. Did billionaires really have trouble meeting women?

Brynnan smiled again. "Well, that makes sense, I guess."

"I had no idea he found the boxes in

Hershel's boat. Hopefully Hershel can give us some clues on the origin of the artifacts."

Brynnan hoped so too. The drive to Hershel Kade's home was less than ten minutes. Brynnan enjoyed looking at the historic homes and modern mansions along the tree-lined esplanades of River Oaks.

"Marsten, did you live near here before you moved to the ranch?" asked Brynnan.

"Yes, I lived a few blocks from Hershel."

"Why did you decide to move?" she asked. "Oh, several reasons. The bluebonnets in the spring. Less traffic. And I was getting tired of dealing with the flooding in Houston."

Everyone in Houston was tired of the flooding. Sick and tired. And no one likes traffic. So, it was a reasonable sounding answer, but Brynnan and Jack both felt Marsten was holding something back.

Jack's phone rang just as they pulled into Hershel's driveway. He took the call as they exited the car and hung back while Marsten walked up to the door. Brynnan didn't want to intrude on the phone call, but she slowed her steps to keep a little closer to Jack. For reasons she didn't understand, she felt a little safer next to Jack than next to her uncle.

The conversation was short. Jack ended the call and caught up to Brynnan. He locked eyes with her. She could tell he had news, and the look in his eyes worried her and warmed her all at the same time.

"Brynnan, everything's fine, but you should know, Nesser made bail."

"What? He's out already?" She hated how much that scared her.

"Yes. Even though we have our theories, all

they charged him with was trespassing and attempted breaking and entering. And considering the deep pockets he's apparently associated with, I'm sure he easily made bail."

"Yeah, ok, I know that makes sense, I just didn't think it would happen so fast."

"Hey," he took her hand and squeezed it, "everything's going to be fine. Trust me."

She gave him a smile, drawing strength from his touch.

He let his gentle grip linger a few seconds, pulling her thoughts to his warm embrace and his kiss... Her face flushed.

This feels so real. He *feels so real. Am I ready for this?*

They walked up to Hershel's front porch with Brynnan's head spinning. Nesser was out of jail, they still had no answers, and Jack McKerrick was making her feel safe and terrified all at the same time. *Oh Lord, help me now.*

Hershel's home was just as impressive as Victor's, also built in the nineteen-thirties, but with its' own distinct flair. A Mediterranean style home, it boasted a three-tiered fountain at least ten feet tall, centered in the front circle drive, guarded by four stone-carved lions.

No silver haired butler greeted them. Instead, Hershel's front door flew open just as they were walking up the front steps.

Hershel himself stood in the doorway.

"Marsten?" Hershel said. He looked confused. "Good morning, cousin. I didn't know you were in town. Why on earth are you in one of Victor's cars?"

His tone wasn't rude, but it wasn't warm either.

Introductions were made and Hershel, with more politeness this time, invited his unexpected guests inside.

The Mediterranean design continued elegantly through the entry and into a two-story living room. Brynnan took in the dark wood ceiling, white stucco walls and fireplace. She felt like she was visiting an opulent seaside Italian villa.

As before, Marsten got right to the point. He explained all about Nesser attempting a break-in via the tunnels, their suspicion he was after the artifacts that previously belonged to Hershel, and even about Nesser causing Brynnan's parents' accident.

Hershel listened without interrupting. Jack watched him intently.

When Marsten finished, Hershel took a deep breath, shaking his head slowly. "That's all so terrible, I just can't believe it. Miss Marsh, I'm very sorry for your loss."

"Thank you," Brynnan replied quietly.

"But I'm afraid I don't know anything helpful about your situation," Hershel said.

"But the boxes," said Brynnan, "they belonged to you, before you sold your boat to your cousinde. Do you have any idea what could be especially valuable about the contents of those boxes?"

"Well, yes, I mean, valuable to me, at least. I'd appreciate having them back—the ones in your possession, if you don't mind. You see, I was having some remodeling done in my home not long ago, and one of my staff put those boxes in the boat, for safe keeping during the remodel. They didn't know I was about to sell the boat and I didn't realize which boxes they stored there. It was really just an unfortunate case of miscommunication."

Brynnan felt suspicious. Hershel's story sounded very rehearsed. But how could it be—he didn't know they were coming, did he? "Your cousin, Victor, said he mentioned the boxes to you after he bought the boat and you said you didn't want them."

"Yes, I did. Like I said, it was a misunderstanding. I thought the boxes stored in the boat were a different set of boxes."

Marsten kept quiet. Jack wasn't sure his boss was on any better footing with Hershel than he was with Victor. This was a complicated family. But if Marsten didn't have any questions for Hershel, he certainly did.

"If you don't mind me asking, sir, what in the boxes is so important to you? Brynnan and I were looking at the contents of one of the boxes last night and she didn't see anything that seemed especially valuable."

Jack didn't know if anyone else noticed, but when he mentioned they'd looked through the contents of the box, Hershel's muscles tensed. The man was nervous.

"Oh, nothing of exceptional, historical value," Hershel was trying to sound casual, "they're just some items of sentimental value."

He offered no more. Which, in itself, was suspicious. This guy was getting on Jack's nerves.

Marsten finally spoke. "I understand. Which items do you need returned? I was planning on sending them all to the museum, but if there's something you wish to keep, I'll have it sent to you by all means."

Brynnan was pleased with her uncle's question.

Hershel hesitated. He looked like he was trying to make a decision. "Oh, it's not much, just a few handkerchiefs. They were a gift from a friend. I never meant for them to be mixed up with the other artifacts. If it wouldn't be too much trouble…"

"Of course, Hershel, that's no trouble, but there's still the matter of Mr. Nesser. Why would he go to so much trouble to retrieve the contents of the box?"

Hershel's polite act was fading. Irritation laced his words.

"How do you know that's what's going on? I understand what you explained earlier, but you don't really know what happened in Austin, or why someone tried to break into your house. The presence of the boxes could be a coincidence."

"I find that unlikely," Marsten said.

Color rose in Hershel's face. "I didn't hire Nesser, no matter what you think. I'd appreciate the handkerchiefs back, but they're only sentimental, like I said. There's no conspiracy here. Nothing that has anything to do with *me* that is." He looked pointedly at Brynnan.

"What?" she asked. "What do you think I have to do with this?"

"Well dear," he said, not so sweetly, "these incidents seem to involve you, or your family. Maybe your mother's family has more to do with this than the Kades. I'm sure they have plenty of men like Nesser on their payroll."

"That's enough!" Marsten roared at Hershel.

Jack's blood boiled. But his words were ice. "We're done here." He turned to Marsten. "Sir, unless you have more questions, I suggest we continue our quest elsewhere."

"Yes, we should go," he said, glaring at Hershel.

Jack looked at Brynnan. Her deep brown eyes swirled with frustration, hurt and confusion. He needed to get her out of there. "Let's go," he said quietly. She nodded. But before she turned to leave, she looked back at Hershel. Her glare held no fear or defeat, only contempt and fiery determination. Now he *really* needed to get her out of there.

Back at the car, Marsten suggested getting lunch.

"Good idea," said Jack.

Marsten gave the driver directions to a restaurant nearby. Brynnan glared back at the house again.

Jack opened the car door for her. She exhaled and slid into the backseat, her mind still reeling from the conversation with Hershel.

"I'm sorry about that," said Marsten, as the car exited Hershel's front gate, "but I do believe most of that exchange was helpful." He turned to Jack. "What do you think?"

"I agree. I know he's your cousin, sir, but…"

"Don't hold back because he's related to me. I told you, they're a rotten bunch. I don't trust any of them."

"In that case, sir, yes, I agree, he was acting guilty. He was definitely lying, at least part of the time. But that doesn't answer all our questions. If he wanted the handkerchiefs—if that's what this is all about—why not just ask for them casually to begin with? Why hire Nesser? This still doesn't add up. I don't trust Hershel, and I think we need to take a close look at those handkerchiefs, but I'm not convinced he hired Nesser."

Brynnan kept quiet. But there was nothing quiet about her eyes. Jack could see her mind was firing on all cylinders, calculating. Why wasn't she spilling her thoughts? Was she afraid to talk in front of Marsten? Afraid to talk in front of *him*? Why did the idea of Brynnan not trusting him crush him so much? He didn't want to think about that. They all needed a break. Lunch was a good idea.

Unfortunately, lunch didn't lift the tension.

Marsten announced some unexpected news while they ate their salads. Some news he seemed to think was of little consequence. Neither Jack nor Brynnan took it lightly.

"I intended to mention earlier, that I called Bobby Alesi last night."

Jack nearly choked on the iced tea he was drinking. "Sir? You called Bobby Alesi?" He looked at Brynnan. She was as stunned as he was.

"Yes, I put it off as long as I could. I don't speak to him often, for obvious reasons, but I wanted to see if anyone had threatened to harm his family lately. If his enemies wanted to hurt Bobby by targeting his family, they'd make it clear. But he said he hadn't received any threats or warnings of any kind."

Brynnan was staring at Marsten like he had three heads. "I... I didn't know you ever talked to him.

How do you know him?"

For a fraction of a second Jack was sure Marsten had said more than he'd planned to. Was he hiding something? Or just trying to dance around explaining harsh realities to Brynnan? Either way, Jack was very interested in how Marsten was going to answer Brynnan's question.

"Sweetheart, there are many things from the past that you deserve to know about, but for today, I'll just say Jonathan and Rachel and I were very close long before you were born, even before they were married. I met Bobby Alesi a very long time ago. I'm not saying he's a good man. He's not. He's spent his entire adult life making money by various illegal means. However," Marsten sighed, sadness in his eyes, "he did love your mother very much. I can't deny that. And he loves you. That may sound strange to you, but it's the truth."

Brynnan was speechless. She had so many questions. So. Many. Questions. But she couldn't find her voice.

Marsten continued. "He did come to the funeral. He decided not to approach you. I hope you understand, it doesn't bother me a bit that he keeps his distance from you. Like I said, he's not a good person. But I can't lie to you and say he didn't love your mother, or that he doesn't love you, because I know he does. And that's why I knew he would tell me if he had any knowledge of threats against you."

Jack watched Brynnan try to grasp Marsten's revelation and cryptic explanation. Not speaking. She finally looked at him. Her wide eyes clearly asking, 'did you hear what he just said?'

Marsten changed the subject by discussing the

plans for the rest of their day. Jack participated in the conversation. Brynnan did not.

They decided to forgo visiting Marsten's uncle. Marsten was sure his only input would be about the history of the tunnels, and while that could prove interesting, it likely wouldn't shine any light on their mystery.

Marsten's assistant, Cass Green, texted during lunch that the third cousin living in Houston was vacationing in Italy. They could call him later if they felt they needed to, but that scratched another visit off the list.

The drive back to Victor's house was quiet. Too quiet.

Brynnan's silence was eating at Jack more than he cared to admit to himself. She'd only made eye contact with him once since Marsten's little speech. Maybe, when they got back to the ranch, she would tell him what she was thinking. But what if she didn't? What if she didn't want to open up to him again? She'd had time to think since last night. She may be regretting letting him kiss her. He'd probably crossed a line too soon and scared her. Stupid.

He shoved his worries down. Brynnan would talk when she was ready. He needed to concentrate on keeping her safe. The Kade cousins had given him plenty to think about.

CHAPTER NINE

When they arrived back at Victor's home, they had no desire to go inside. The helipad was accessible from the side of the house, so they decided to walk around to Marsten's waiting helicopter rather than walking through the house and interacting with Victor. Marsten's cousins were worse than Brynnan had imagined.

So much about Marsten's revelation at lunch had her confused, curious, and even angry—angry about being kept in the dark about so much from the people she should have been able to trust the most. And Marsten had eluded to more things he hadn't yet shared. What more could there be?

She loved her uncle. She couldn't refute that. And didn't regret it. He'd been there for her, cared for her, when she'd needed him most. But loving and trusting were two different things. She wasn't sure how far she could trust Marsten Kade. This loving, caring man who'd held her hand through her darkest days had so many secrets. So. Many. Secrets.

And she hardly knew how to process the Kade cousins she'd met that day. Victor was downright disturbing, but the question really nagging at her was, how on earth did Hershel know anything about her mother's family? Her mother was, technically, his cousin's half-brother's wife. What were the odds that they'd ever met?

The events of the day were giving her a headache. And figuring out how the Kades knew the Alesis probably wouldn't help her figure out who was after the artifacts, or her.

Hershel and Victor had both acted guilty. She didn't know which cousin she liked least. And she agreed with Jack—as much as she wished they could just blame Hershel or Victor and it all be over, the pieces didn't fit. They had proof of nothing. How were either of them connected to Nesser? And why? Why were her parents killed? Why was he under her floor? She visibly shuddered.

"You okay?" asked Jack.

No, I'm not at all okay.

"Yeah, I guess," she answered. She knew she wasn't convincing. But if she leaned on him right now, she'd fall apart. And she wasn't going to do that in front of Marsten. She ached to be alone with Jack, so they could discuss everything, and she could vent her frustrations. But maybe that was unfair. She didn't want to expect too much—didn't want to take advantage of his compassion.

Her family, on *both* sides, was crooked and full of secrets. Jack didn't deserve to be pulled into this drama. He had to deal with some of it on a professional level, as Marsten's security, but he didn't need all that dysfunction in his personal life. The times he talked about his own family, she sensed the warmth and love that kept them knit together—like a Norman Rockwell painting. He deserved a woman from a stable, caring family like his own. Not an organized crime family, and... whatever the Kades were.

They spotted Marsten's pilot doing a preflight check as they approached the helipad.

Jack's voice pulled her from her thoughts. "You sure you're okay?"

"Yes," she lied again.

As they took the steps up to the helipad, she permitted her eyes to meet his. "Really, I'm fine. I'm ready to get back and take another look at those handkerchiefs, in case there's something more to them."

He gave a nod and a subtle smile. She didn't miss the worry in his eyes. Was it for her or the whole situation? Probably both. She wanted to say something encouraging but, couldn't think of anything. She decided to simply return his smile.

But she didn't get the chance. Strong arms wrapped around her neck and jerked her backward off the steps.

CHAPTER TEN

Jack sensed motion on his left and was already reaching for his weapon when Brynnan was grabbed by someone to his right. Their attackers had concealed themselves in the dense foliage around the steps to the helipad. It all happened in about two seconds. Now, two gunmen trained their weapons on Marsten and Jack, while a third kept Marsten's pilot from getting any ideas. Nesser's arm was around Brynnan's neck, and he held a gun to her head.

Jack pointed his gun at Nesser.

Nesser smiled. "You're out manned and out gunned, Cowboy, lower your weapon."

Jack kept his gun trained on Nesser. "Let. Her. Go.," he said, deadly threat laced his words.

Nesser let out a sick laugh. "No, I don't think so."

Jack glanced at Brynnan. She was scared. The fear in her eyes clawed every nerve in his chest.

"Stay calm," he told her. "Everything's going

to be fine."

"I'm the one in charge, Cowboy. 'Everything's gonna be fine' only if you do what I say. Now you listen. Here's how this is going to go. You and Marsten get in the chopper. Go back to his ranch, get the handkerchiefs. You bring them back here, and we'll exchange the handkerchiefs for the girl."

Marsten glared at Nesser. "The handkerchiefs? All this for the handkerchiefs? This isn't necessary! We were going to give them back to Hershel as soon as possible!"

Jack responded to Marsten's comment, keeping his eyes on Nesser, his voice even. "They're not working for Hershel."

"Well, aren't you bright," said Nesser. "Now, if you call the police, or refuse to cooperate, you'll get the girl back in pieces." He shot a look at Marsten. "Your boss can tell you, he knows we're serious."

Realization dawned on Marsten. He nodded. "Don't hurt her Nesser. We understand." He looked at Jack. "He's right, Jack. They're serious. I've never met Mr. Nesser before, but I recognize two of these other vermin. A Kade is behind this. Most likely Victor. And they're not bluffing. They've…they've hurt people before."

Jack kept his gun aimed at Nesser, saying nothing.

"Please, Jack, cooperate." Marsten's voice was strained. "The only thing that matters right now is making sure Brynnan doesn't get hurt."

"Listen to him, Cowboy," said Nesser.

Jack locked eyes with Brynnan. "Trust me," he said, in the strongest, calmest voice she'd ever heard.

She gave a shaky nod, too frightened to speak.

She couldn't believe how scared she was. After the horrific experiences in her teens, then surrendering her life to God in college, she'd grown so much stronger, fearless at times. Even two years ago, when she was in the mall parking lot and a guy tried to grab her purse, she shoved her keys at his eyes, kicked him in the crotch, and got away, with her purse, leaving him moaning on the ground.

But. This. Was. Different.

Four men with guns. And the one with his arm around her neck was responsible for her parents' deaths. The thought weakened her. Her legs wobbled.

"Toss your gun. And then, you and Marsten walk to the chopper. Slowly," said Nesser.

Jack lowered his weapon. "I'm not going to shoot," he said, slipping the gun into his waistband. "But I'm not giving you my weapon." He held his hands in the air, signaling his partial submission, sans handing over his gun. "We'll get your precious handkerchiefs, but if you hurt her," he lowered his voice, stepping closer to Nesser, "I *promise*, you will regret it."

Nesser growled. "Get on the chopper. And keep your hands in the air until you're gone."

Jack felt Brynnan's eyes boring into him. Pleading with him. Was she hoping he'd shoot Nesser, while his arm was around her neck? That wasn't going to happen.

Or was she begging him not to leave her? She couldn't possibly know how much the fear on her face was affecting him. What it was doing to him. How it was hollowing him out and setting him on fire. But he needed to focus. For her sake. And

Marsten's.

Nesser tightened his sweaty grip. Brynnan winced.

"Nesser, calm down, don't hurt her," said Marsten, uncharacteristic desperation in his voice, "we're going." He started to move toward the helicopter.

Wait, no! Were they really going to leave her?

Hot terror burned through her, igniting a blaze of fear, fanning the flames of panic—until she saw the stone-cold resolve on Jack's face.

He's going to do something. I can tell. He won't let these guys win. He won't leave me.

Jack's eyes bore through her, the intensity in his gaze smothering her panic, bolstering her. He stood there looking every bit the hero, her fierce protector. She started to breathe again.

"Bryn," he said quietly, "please trust me."

His tone soothed her. Which was unreal. That his voice could calm her while she had a gun to her head. He'd never called her 'Bryn' before. No one had. She felt a new intimacy in that single syllable. His gaze held hers and she prayed he could see trust in her eyes. Her trust in him.

She did trust him. And she was all-in with whatever plan he was hatching—she just wished she knew exactly what he was thinking—she wanted to be ready for—

But he walked away.

The scene morphed into a slow-motion nightmare—Nesser's gun still pressing mercilessly against her skull, she watched Jack board.

The helicopter lifted from the helipad.

And Marsten, Jack, and her hope of rescue disappeared beyond the trees.

She tried to deny what she was seeing. But it was useless.

Finally, she let the tears fall.

Nesser zip tied Brynnan's hands behind her back, and barked orders to the other three gunmen.

"Go back into the house. Make sure everything's locked up. All the doors and windows. Then keep an eye on the security cameras. I'm going to stash our guest. I'll call to report that everything went smoothly, then meet up with you in a few minutes."

Nesser kicked Brynnan's tote bag she'd dropped deep into the bushes, gripped her arm, tighter than necessary—her will to run took off with the helicopter—and led her into Victor Kade's house.

Jerked forward by Nesser's vise-like hand, faint, terrified, she stumbled down the long hallway—the same long hallway where, only hours earlier, she had to bite her lip to keep from laughing at Jack's humor. Now he was gone. Left her behind.

She knew the overwhelming odds had favored Nesser and his men, but she still felt abandoned.

There was probably nothing Jack or Marsten could have done. It was stupid, naïve, to feel so optimistic when she'd looked at Jack. *But, for a moment, he looked so determined, so invincible, I thought...*

Nesser pulled her through a second hallway

and into a large bedroom. He pushed her to the floor near the bed and produced a roll of duct tape. "Stay still, and this will go easier for you." His cold voice hissed the threat.

That's when the déjà vu coiled around her and started to squeeze the air from her lungs.

Again. It was happening again. Wrists bound. Duct tape. Threats. No, no, no!

He bound her wrists, still zip-tied, to the leg of the bed so quickly that she was sure this wasn't the first time he'd held a prisoner.

Her newest nightmare, very alive and very real, engulfed her. She felt dizzy.

In another few seconds, he'd duct taped her ankles together.

"Now, Miss, you stay here," he said, covering her mouth with a final piece of tape. "You stay still, and quiet, and you just may survive this."

He stood. His gaze traveled her body, head to toe. His hands stayed on his hips, but his expression was so disgusting she felt violated. A smile crawled across his face. She wanted to vomit.

Don't get sick with tape over your mouth. That would be bad. Hold it together.

"I'll be back to check on you in a few minutes. Don't miss me too much." He laughed at his own joke and walked out of the room.

Panic seized her. Her breaths came faster. Her heartbeat pounded in her ears. Tears stung her eyes. *This can't be happening. Not again.* Images from the past attacked her so forcibly she almost felt the blows. Felt them pull her hair. Heard the curses. Smelled their breath. Tasted her own fear.

Her very real present danger, compounded with her terrorized past, threatened to overwhelm her.

God! She tried to pray but, like the night her parents were killed, she wasn't capable of reverent maxims. *Help! Help! Help!* She had no other words. But this time, she knew God was there. She reminded herself she wasn't truly alone. She focused on controlling her breathing, and a verse she'd memorized years ago floated to the front of her consciousness. *He is my refuge and my fortress, my God, in whom I trust.*

She repeated the scripture over and over as her breathing regulated.

Trust. That's what she needed to do. Trust that God would protect her, be her refuge and fortress, in ways only God could.

The men might come for her soon. Nesser may try to hurt her. But God would be with her. She didn't know if God would keep the men away, or sustain her to survive what lay ahead, but either way, she had God's peace and power on her side this time. And Nesser and his men couldn't do anything about that.

She felt calmer. Stronger. Her mind cleared.

Okay, I probably only have a few minutes, I need to make the most of it.

She searched her surroundings for something to cut her bindings, and her attention paused on an ornate cabinet against a wall, maybe five or six feet from the foot of the bed. Rows of books sat on the bottom shelves of the cabinet behind glass doors. *Glass.*

Could she stretch herself far enough to reach the doors?

Her hands were bound to a leg of the bed, but her feet, though bound to each other, were free of the bed. She scooted herself to a prone position attempting to lengthen her body as far as she could. Her toes hit glass. Yes! This might work.

She craned her neck, eyeing her goal. This was the absolute worst time to be wearing sandals. At least they weren't flip flops. It didn't matter anyway, she'd rather have cuts on her feet than be sitting in this room when Nesser came back. She gritted her teeth, took a deep breath, and kicked the glass as hard as she could. Her effort was rewarded with a crack.

She needed to hurry. If she made too much noise, Nesser or one of the others might hear her. She kicked again.

This time a large chunk of glass broke away and fell into the cabinet. That wouldn't help her. She needed a piece to fall out onto the floor. She repositioned her feet through the hole she'd made so the straps of her sandals pressed against the glass from the inside of the cabinet and pulled her feet toward her with as much force as she could. Another chunk of glass popped off the cabinet door, and this time, landed on the floor.

Too early to celebrate. Using the piece of glass to cut herself free was probably going to be very difficult.

And it was.

It took so much longer than she'd imagined. *In the movies things like this take about ten seconds.* But this wasn't a movie. She worked and worked on sawing the duct tape with her little piece of glass, accidentally cutting herself no less than three times, before she was free of the bed. Then she worked on the zip ties.

Then her ankles.

By the time she was free to stand, the muscles in her bleeding hands were cramping. But she was free.

She ripped the duct tape from her mouth, stifling a yelp. *Wow, that hurt.*

Lifting up a quick prayer of thanks, she turned to the door. She prayed for protection. For lots of protection.

CHAPTER ELEVEN

The conversation in the helicopter was brief. As soon as the skids left Victor's helipad, Jack turned to the pilot. "Find somewhere close to put me down. Four or Six blocks from the house is good enough."

"You sure about that?" asked the pilot. A minute ago may have been his first time to be held at gunpoint, but to his credit, he wasn't panicking.

"Yes. Just get me down there."

The pilot gave a thumbs up.

Jack read the worry in his boss's eyes. "Who am I dealing with, sir? The men you recognized, what's their background?"

Marsten's features hardened. "Mercenaries. But I don't know anything about the kind of training they've had, if that's what you mean. I don't have a shred of proof, but I'm certain they're responsible for torturing the sister of one of Victor's competitors a couple of years ago."

Jack's gut fisted. "What?"

"The details don't matter now, but yes, these men are very dangerous. They're...they're not bluffing."

Jack leaned forward, his elbows on his knees, and ran his hands over his face. He still didn't understand the big picture, but he knew this was about more than handkerchiefs. The knife-guy at Professor Krupp's house had specifically wanted Brynnan, not just the handkerchiefs.

And her parents were dead.

He didn't hold any real hope of an exchange. They'd keep her alive just long enough to use her.

Her frightened eyes held his mind captive for a few breaths. He wanted to reach for her, back at the helipad. Wanted to pull her away from Nesser, pull her to himself and never let go. But it could've gotten her killed. He wanted to shoot Nesser, but again, it could've...

A piercing agony burned in his hollow chest. Familiar, yet more intense than before. He was more afraid for Brynnan now than he had been for himself in the small, dark cell all those years ago. Brynnan... He could almost feel her soft lips on his, her arms clinging to him, as if...

Stop. That's not helping. Tamp down the fear. Compartmentalize. She's counting on me. Focus on a plan.

Rescuing a hostage was something he'd done before. More than once. But he hadn't been emotionally involved like this. He prayed an earnest, raw, humble prayer. For wisdom and protection. For Brynnan. For them both.

After a few seconds, he sat up straight, confidence and determination pulsing through him. He gave Marsten instructions to return to the ranch, get the handkerchiefs, and head back toward Victor's, but to stay in contact with him via text.

"Don't land at Victor's unless you hear from

me first," Jack instructed. "Hopefully, I'll have Brynnan out and we'll be away from the house before then, and you won't need to land. But just in case, bring the handkerchiefs—we may need to exchange them for Brynnan. We need Nesser to think we're cooperating."

"Do you think it's too dangerous to call the police?" Marsten asked, looking sick with worry.

"I don't want to involve the local police just yet. They would need to know the whole story and we don't have time for that. I need to get to Brynnan *now*. Plus, we can't risk spooking Nesser—one siren could cost us. I'll contact the FBI, but they won't be able to get here fast enough. I'm not waiting."

Marsten fixed a look on Jack that spoke volumes. He wanted Brynnan back. At all costs.

Jack checked his weapon and reached for the door. "If you don't hear from me in thirty minutes, call in the cavalry."

When the helicopter touched down at a park six blocks from Victor's house, Jack was still calculating a plan. And several contingencies.

He would use the element of surprise to his favor as much as possible. In fact, he'd very much like to avoid confronting Nesser or his men altogether. Just get in, find Brynnan, get out. But he knew that was a lot to hope for.

He called his dad while he jogged the six blocks. He suggested Jack wait for back up. But his suggestion wasn't very adamant. Jack sensed his dad knew time was precious and that Brynnan would fare better the sooner Jack could get to her. His dad would reach out to his FBI resources. And a friend. They both promised to text any updates, and Jack ended the call.

Two minutes later, Jack saw Victor's house come into view a half block away. His phone vibrated. A text from his dad read: Friend on the way. ETA 20 min.

Good. At least the exfil plan was taking shape.

Now, he just needed to breach the house and locate Brynnan while avoiding all the cameras and gunmen.

He prayed for Brynnan again. And a miracle.

Brynnan wondered if she was walking in circles. The house was huge. And dark. Victor apparently wasn't a fan of natural light. And she didn't dare flip any light switches.

She could hear men's voices toward the front of the house, so she tried to look for a way out the back without being seen. After a few turns, a door framed in windows appeared. Definitely an exterior door. Maybe it led to the backyard.

She stiffened at the sound of footfalls. Someone large was tramping down the hallway near her. A hall of bedrooms was behind her, the exterior door in front of her. Rushing for the door would expose her to whoever was coming down the hall. But she was *so close*. Should she run, or hide?

Muscular arms pulled her off her feet and a hand covered her mouth, making the decision for her.

She started to kick, until she registered the gentle shushing in her ear. Then a faint, "It's me." The arms eased and she spun around to face Jack. Elation ballooned inside her, but there wasn't time for relief.

He pulled her into the nearest bedroom and froze near the door, listening.

The heavy footfalls pounded closer.

Arm around her waist, Jack guided Brynnan into a closet with him as fast as humanly possible. He shut the closet door and moved her behind him. She instinctively knew not to move a muscle. Or was too scared to.

The movement from the hallway entered the bedroom.

Of all the bedrooms...this one, really? You had to come in here?

They heard him flip on the lights and a sliver of brightness reached them from the bottom of the door.

They heard a drawer open and close. A large zipper, maybe on a suitcase. He was looking for something.

Oh, please, not the closet. Whatever he's looking for, please don't let it be in the closet.

The terror of being found pricked at her every nerve. She was scared to death of what they might do to her, to Jack. But Jack *was* here now. He'd come back for her. He hadn't had time to go back to the ranch first—he hadn't left, she knew that now. Part of her wanted to throw herself at him, lose herself in his arms and never leave. But she knew any movement would draw the attention of whoever-he-was in the bedroom, and that could end very tragically. Survival instinct won out. She remained frozen.

Jack was tense, alert, with a trained air of calm about him. Yeah, this was full on soldier mode. She stood behind him and studied his outline in the near-dark closet. She'd appreciated his broad shoulders and muscular build before, but not in the same way—in that moment, she was just glad that wall of muscle was between her and the bad guy. She had no idea when he'd retrieved his gun, but it was out, and he was ready.

More steps sounded in the hall, and a second man walked in.

"What are you doing?" he asked.

"Getting the extra burners." That was definitely Nesser's voice. "I'll take two and you carry two. Keep them on you. We might need to leave quickly. If I think, for a second, that Marsten or his security guy called the cops, we'll take the girl and worry about the handkerchiefs later. I have some ideas about that. We'll get this wrapped up quickly one way or the other. Victor is sure that with the girl and her parents all out of the picture, that should do it."

"I wouldn't mention that part to Ricky anymore. About the parents, I mean. He's still ticked about how you handled that in Austin. He wanted to use Rachel—"

"I know, I know! He and his buddies will just have to get over it. This was about getting paid for a job, not any kind of revenge," said Nesser.

"Hey, I'm with you. I just wanna get paid. All I'm saying is, watch out for Ricky. You two aren't on the same page. He didn't get to use Rachel, so he's not going to go for just dumping the girl. He'll want to use her against Bobby instead. He seems to think he could double his money—get paid by Kade, then milk Bobby for the girl before he kills her."

"Keep your thumb on Ricky then. We're keeping this as simple as possible from here on out. It shouldn't have dragged out this much."

"You want to just kill her now? Might be easier. She might be trouble if we need to move fast."

"I know, but we need her as insurance. We don't have the handkerchiefs yet. Victor hasn't thought all this through. He's paying me to take care of the details. So, we hang on to her until we get the handkerchiefs."

"Ok, but I don't like the idea of dragging her around with us. She'll be trouble if she's conscious. Or she'll be a pain to carry if we knock her out. I want to just finish it here and get to the airport."

"I know, I know. Look, this isn't my first job. Don't worry about it. Marsten's scared. I saw it in his eyes. He'll bring the handkerchiefs. He won't chance it."

"Alright. Fine. I'm going to double-check our..."

The door opened and the voices faded down the hall.

Jack slid his gun into his waistband and pivoted in the small space to face Brynnan. "Are you hurt?"

"N... no."

"We need to move fast. They'll know you're gone in a minute or so, I'm sure they'll check. You ready to run?"

She wanted to say yes, but Nesser's words kept her paralyzed. He'd practically confessed to murdering her parents, and his intention to do the same to her. And she still didn't know why. *Why was this happening?*

"Brynnan?" Jack gently gripped her upper

arms and pulled her closer to his face. "Brynnan, I'm sorry. I'm so sorry this happened. But, We. Have. To. Go. Can you run?"

"Yes, I... yes, I'm good." Did she just lie? She felt so weak and scared. Could she run? Could she move?

"Ok, stay close." He retrieved his weapon, edged the door open and stepped into the bedroom. She found herself following him. She tried to wrangle her thoughts—lock away all the fears and 'what-ifs' and just follow Jack. She could do that. Probably.

They moved to the bedroom door. Jack paused to ascertain whether the hallway was clear.

No sound.

He glanced back at Brynnan, relieved she was following so close. He'd been afraid a moment ago that she was paralyzed with fear. He couldn't blame her, but they had a much better chance of making a clean escape if he didn't have to carry her.

He assessed her for the first time in the light, and his eyes bulged when he saw the cuts on her hands.

"It's okay," she mouthed. "Let's go."

Something simultaneously beautiful and painful wrapped around his heart and squeezed. He saw the bloody cuts, and where the zip-ties had rubbed her skin raw—bindings she obviously escaped on her own. She still looked terrified, but there was also courage and trust in her eyes. The sight shifted emotions inside him he didn't have time to process. He had to get her away from Nesser. Now.

"Stay close," he whispered.

Silently, they crept down the hallway. He

needed to make a decision. He didn't know the location of Nesser or the others, so they were taking a chance with any of the routes he considered.

The plan he chose wasn't great, but given what he knew, it was the best option.

He hurried Brynnan down another hallway about ten feet, stopped, led her into a guest bathroom and shut the door. He texted Marsten that Brynnan was with him and not to return to Victor's. She looked confused and a little doubtful until he stood on the toilet and unlocked a small window. He knew if the men in the house were mercenaries worth their salt, they would see them escaping on security cameras. But escaping out of this wing of the house should give them a decent head start, and their ride should be close by now. He hoped.

"Opening this window might set off an alarm, I don't know. But even if it doesn't, they may spot us on cameras while we're climbing out or leaving the property. So, once I raise the window, we move fast."

"Okay."

Just before he lifted the window, he pressed his lips to hers. Hard. Fast. Fierce. It lasted two seconds, but it felt important. Like he needed to.

They heard yelling in the house. Nesser knew she'd escaped. He threw the window open. "Go, now!"

She didn't expect to go first, but between the look on Jack's face and the yelling in the house, she decided there wasn't time to discuss the plan. She stepped up on the toilet, pulled herself through the window and dropped to her feet in a flowerbed.

"Run! I'm right behind you!" Jack's command

was urgent, but quiet.

She took off but, had no idea where she was going. She headed for a grouping of mature post oaks. She could wait behind the trees until Jack caught up.

The sound of gunfire jerked a yelp from her lungs and she nearly tripped, but she made it to the first tree and hid behind the massive trunk.

They're shooting at us. Fantastic.

Her pulse pounded in her ears so loudly she couldn't hear Jack coming. Suddenly, he flew through her peripheral vision, grabbed her hand and kept them running faster than Brynnan thought she was capable. They navigated through the yards of several large estates before Jack pulled her into the shadows behind a large greenhouse.

She tried to breathe.

He checked his phone.

"He's here," Jack said, smiling for the first time since meeting Darlington.

"Who?"

"A friend." He took her hand again. "This way."

She didn't tell him how badly her hand was hurting. If he knew, he might let go. And she wasn't ready for that.

They jogged back up to a residential street and approached a black SUV slowing to a stop. Jack seemed to recognize the driver and gave a thumbs up. He opened the back passenger's side door for Brynnan. She hopped in the stranger's car and watched Jack tense.

He was looking down the road behind them.

"Go, go, go!" he yelled, jumping practically on

top of her in the backseat. She shifted out from underneath him and slid into the next seat.

"What is it? Did they see us?"

"Yes," he answered. He turned to the driver. "Jonas, floor it! Dark blue sedan on your six. Try to lose them."

"Glad to see you too. Don't worry about those guys. They won't be a problem for long."

Jonas didn't seem a bit nervous about being chased by merciless gunmen. He reminded Brynnan of Buck, except he was closer to Jack's age.

Jack wiped the sweat off his face and rubbed his hands on his jeans. "Glad to see you Jonas. I was hoping Dad could reach you. You really saved us. One of my contingency plans involved jumping in Buffalo Bayou."

Jonas raised his brows. "Okaaaay. Wouldn't have been my first choice either. But we're about a klick east of there now if you wanna take a dip to cool off. You look hot."

"No thanks, we'll stick with outrunning them on the road. You think you can lose them in the Houston traffic?"

"I'm offended you have to ask. I'm also offended that you haven't introduced me."

"Sorry, but watch the road, and—"

"Ma'am, please don't mind him," Jonas said, smiling at Brynnan in the rearview mirror. "He has terrible manners. My name is Jonas. Jonas Rorke."

"Hello, Jonas. I'm Brynnan. Thank you for getting us out of there."

"Pleased to make your acquaintance, ma'am." He tipped an imaginary hat.

Jack rolled his eyes. "When you're done

flirting, maybe we could lose these guys. They're still two cars back."

Brynnan tried to take comfort in the fact that neither Jack or Jonas seemed panicked, but the proximity of the sedan was unnerving her.

Jack looked behind them and watched the blue sedan maneuver a turn way too quickly. "I can't believe they found a car so fast."

"What do you mean?" asked Brynnan.

"I disabled all the vehicles I could find on the property before I came in the house. Either they had this one parked down the street, or they stole one from a neighbor. Doesn't matter now. We just need to lose them."

"Don't worry. Just sit back, relax, and let me do my thing," said Jonas. He made a quick turn. "On second thought, you should probably put on your seatbelts. But I'll get rid of these guys. No problem."

"Guys?" asked Brynnan, her sore hands gingerly handling the seatbelt buckle. "Can you tell how many are in the car?"

"Yeah," answered Jonas. "I got a good look a second ago. At least two ugly dudes. Could be another in the backseat. Not sure about that."

Jack retrieved his weapon, keeping his eyes on the blue sedan.

Jonas eyed him through the rearview mirror. "Steady, Jack. I'm not going to let them get that close."

"That'll be fine with me."

Jonas jerked the wheel to the left and back to the right, weaving through the evening work traffic. Jack decided the seatbelt was a good idea.

He looked down to grab the buckle and

noticed Brynnan's hands again. "Let me see," he said quietly.

"It's not that bad. It was my fault. I used a piece of glass to cut off the duct tape and zip ties." She shook her head. "Obviously, I'm not very skilled at such things."

Carefully lifting her hands, he examined the cuts. "Jonas, you have a first aid kit in here?"

"Of course. Behind your seat. Everything okay?"

Brynnan sighed. "Yes, I'm fine. Some minor cuts, but they can wait." She threw Jack a pleading look and withdrew her hands. "Can we get somewhere safe first?"

"Okay." He checked behind them again. "Not bad, Jonas. They're eight cars back."

"I'm aware. Your tone sounds skeptical. You want to drive?"

"Are you offering?"

"No. No, I'm not. Just sit tight."

Brynnan started thinking maybe she should have let Jack doctor her hands for a few minutes—that would've been a good distraction from the sedan, or from dwelling on the fact that he wasn't driving. He really wanted to drive.

Jonas seemed very competent though. And confident. She felt like they were in good hands.

Thirty minutes later, Jonas proved himself.

They hadn't seen the blue sedan in the past twenty minutes.

"Okay friends," said Jonas. "I think we're safe now. This has been fun but, where can I drop you? I have plans tonight."

"I'm working on that," said Jack. He looked

down at his phone and sent another text. He'd sent at least a dozen texts while they snaked through the Houston suburbs the last few minutes. "I don't think it's safe to go straight to Marsten's ranch yet. They may try to intercept us there. I'm having Marsten meet us at a safehouse. It's a cabin that belongs to a cousin of mine. No one's there. It sits on plenty of acreage, so Marsten won't have any trouble landing."

"Shouldn't we call the police?" asked Brynnan.

"They've been contacted. And the FBI. My dad and some other agents who have been keeping an eye on Victor will meet us at the cabin. We'll regroup, see what the FBI has to say and decide what to do next."

She nodded, reached for his hand and squeezed it. She wanted him to know she appreciated his protection. Because she did. More than she could articulate.

"Roger that," said Jonas. "Where's this cabin?"

"Northeast of Brenham. Shouldn't take us too long. I'm sending you a pin."

"Got it." He glanced at his phone. "I'll have us there in an hour. Is this one of those cozy cabins with rocking chairs on the front porch?"

Jack pocketed his phone and leaned back in his seat. "I haven't been there in years. I can't promise rocking chairs. It's remote, that's what I like about it. And it has water and electricity, so if we need to stay until tomorrow, it won't be rough. You don't need to stay Jonas, I wouldn't think of keeping you from your evening plans. You've gone above and beyond for us today. I can't calculate how much I owe you now. I won't forget it man, I promise."

"I won't let you forget, buddy, don't you worry," Jonas answered with a hearty laugh, causing Brynnan's anxiety about the whole situation to recede a fraction. It occurred to her that it revealed a lot about Jack that so many friends—Jonas, Cole and Beardall—were willing to walk into dangerous situations with him. She was starting to see why her uncle trusted him so much.

Jack wasn't sure about the cabin having provisions, so they stopped for take-out on the way—a large family style fajita meal. He figured that would give them enough to eat that night and the next morning. Jonas requested extra tortillas, extra guacamole and extra black beans.

"Does this mean you plan on staying?" asked Brynnan.

"Long enough to finish off the guac." He winked at her in the rearview mirror. "I'll definitely stick around until you have plenty of back-up. And I'm interested in the FBI's assessment. I'll hang around as long as you need me."

"What about your big plans tonight?" asked Jack.

"I'm factoring all that in to how much you'll owe me later."

Jack smiled and shook his head. "Fine."

The two-bedroom cabin with wrap-around porch welcomed them with a large, open-concept living area, and a cozy, brick fireplace. Warm and inviting, it made her wish she was arriving for vacation and not hiding from mercenaries.

A second, smaller structure sat about sixty

yards from the cabin near a pond. Jonas decided to "do a little recon," and left Jack and Brynnan alone in the cabin with another tip of his imaginary hat.

"He wants to see if there's any fish in that pond," Jack explained while he helped Brynnan set out the food. "There used to be plenty of poles and tackle in the smaller cabin. Probably still are. He'll be back when he's hungry." He looked at his watch. "The FBI is about thirty minutes out. And your uncle should be here about the same time. Cole is escorting him and bringing the handkerchiefs. I wasn't sure exactly how this was going to end today, so I told Cole to stick with Marsten. They needed to refuel, but they'll be here before dark."

"Good. I know Marsten's worried. Hopefully this will all be over soon." She wondered if she was being too optimistic. The thought drained her.

She opened the containers of salsa, cheese and sour cream and set them next to the chicken fajita meat, grilled onions and peppers. She thought she'd be hungry. But with the adrenaline rush from earlier long gone, and Nesser's menacing words echoing through her mind, she found herself collapsing on the living room sofa instead of piling delicious fixings into a fresh tortilla.

Jack set down the plates he'd found in a cabinet and followed Brynnan into the living area. The pain on her face sliced through him.

Until now, he hadn't permitted himself to stare into her eyes, dwelling on the terror she must have felt being kidnapped. *Again.* He hadn't trusted himself not to come unraveled. So, he'd stayed focused on getting Brynnan out of Victor's house, losing Nesser in the traffic, and finding somewhere safe for them to meet up with the FBI.

But now, guilt and agony for what she'd gone through raked over him. And they were finally alone.

He sank beside her, wrapped his arm around her shoulders and pressed his head to the side of hers, his lips near her ear.

"That shouldn't have happened. None of it. I'm so sorry, Bryn. I'm sorry you went through that," he whispered, raw emotion threatening to crack his voice.

She pulled back to look him in the eyes. "It's not your fault. There were four of them. With guns." She shook her head, as if she could shake away the memory. Her eyes returned to his, moist, but smiling. "But you came. You got me out of there. You brought us here."

She held his gaze, and he knew he'd end up kissing her if he didn't stop himself. Which he needed to do this time. The timing was insane, but she needed to know everything about him before he let their relationship develop into something he couldn't tear himself away from. Though he was probably there already.

The danger and drama of the past two days was pushing them closer together. And Brynnan seemed willing... But she needed to know...

"Brynnan, there are things about me I haven't told you." He pushed some hair away from her face and tucked it behind her ear. "One reason it hurts me so much that you were taken today, and in the past, is because I have some experience in that area. A mission ended badly a few years ago..." Wow. Was he really about to do this? Right now? It could probably wait. Until they weren't being hunted. Until the adrenaline died down.

But something inside him was pushing the issue. Maybe he needed to tell her. Even if he didn't understand why.

"I was taken captive and held for two weeks. I can't talk about the 'where' or 'who,' but that's not the point. The point is, I'm not going to pretend I don't still suffer the effects of that time. I still have nightmares, anxiety at times." He rubbed the back of his neck and prayed for guidance. And realized he should've prayed *before* he started talking.

"This is probably the craziest time to tell you that. But...but when you look at me like that...I can't let you think I have it all together, not like you think I do." He sat before her more vulnerable than he'd ever been in his life.

Huge tears swelled and flowed down her cheeks. Overcome with emotion, she grabbed his arm, stared at him. But he didn't see disappointment in her eyes. Or pity. "I hate that you went through that, Jack. I hate it. I'm so sorry. The evil in this world feels so overwhelming sometimes. I had horrible nightmares for a long time, too. And they might resurface. I know that. But I don't know why. Why does the brain want to dredge up the past?"

She pushed the tears off her face, and he wondered if he was supposed to respond to that question. He hoped not. He didn't have an answer for that one.

She let go of his arm. "I... I didn't mean to go on like that. But I don't know what you're worried about as far as what I think. Because you're a godly man who makes me feel safer than anyone else in the world. You *do* have it together, because I see you leaning on God. And you use the gifts he gave you to protect others. To protect me. You're incredible, Jack."

She seemed to be searching for more words, but not finding any.

None were needed. His revelations hadn't revolted her. Nor did she look at him like he was broken. On the contrary, her eyes were full of respect, trust...and affection. That said enough.

The thump, thump of rotors sounded in the distance.

Unwilling to forfeit their last few moments alone, he pressed his lips to hers, kissing her tenderly. Deeply. Eagerly.

The passion in her response surprised him. And warmed him to his core.

He felt her soft form tremble in his arms.

Moments later, the helicopter's rotors were so loud he was sure it had landed. With excruciating effort, he dialed back the kiss and finally, pressed his forehead to hers. "I think your uncle is here."

Unmoving, she whispered, "I know. We should go."

Reluctantly, he stood, pulling her with him. Not ready to release her from his arms, he kissed her softly once more. She clung to him, showing no interest in leaving his embrace. Grinning, she ran her thumb across his lower lip. Her light touch did nothing to stem the passion he was trying to hold back—but then he realized what she was doing.

"You have a little pink lip gloss on your...I mean, it's a great color, but..." she whispered, clearly amused.

He held her tight against his chest, trying not to laugh—or kiss her—while he let her rub the gloss from his lips.

Until voices outside signaled the end of their privacy.

CHAPTER TWELVE

An hour later, Jonas was refilling his plate for the third time while Marsten, Jack, his dad, two other FBI agents, and Cole sat around the massive dining table discussing the days' events, and their next move.

Brynnan leaned over a rustic coffee table in the living area studying the handkerchiefs, determined to figure out why Victor or Hershel would want them so desperately.

She enjoyed meeting Jack's dad, Ethan McKerrick, when he and the other two agents arrived. The wisdom in his eyes reassured her, as did his quiet strength. He reminded her of Jack. He insisted she call him 'Ethan' and commended her bravery over the past few days.

She told herself this wasn't a 'meeting the parents' scenario, but she was admittedly relieved at the warmth of Ethan's compliments, and the smile they evoked from Jack.

She kneeled beside the coffee table and stared at the puzzle before her. Analyzing every square inch of the handkerchiefs, she hoped for some clue about their origin or value. Each one had seemingly random, hand-stitched decorative lines and shapes. She scrutinized them from every angle, front and back. Nothing stood out. Then she stacked them on top of each other with each one completely unfolded.

Well, that's kind of interesting. The handkerchiefs are so thin the stitching shows through... An idea started forming. She took the stack of handkerchiefs over to a nearby lamp and removed the shade. Holding the stack up near the bulb, her pulse quickened. She reoriented two of the handkerchiefs, then a third, and held the stack up against the bare bulb again.

"Jack! Can I borrow your phone?" she called out, racing over to the table. Her sudden burst, excited volume, and the fact she was running, earned her a crowd of startled expressions. "Sorry," she offered to the group, then looked expectantly at Jack.

"Sure." He handed her his phone. "Did you figure out what they are?"

"Maybe. I need to look up a few things." She grabbed the phone without further explanation and ran back to the lamp. She was vaguely aware of all eyes around the table following her back to the living area, but she couldn't take the time to explain yet. Besides, she might be wrong. She prayed she could access the research she needed using Jack's cell phone, without Wi-Fi. She heard the discussion around the dining table recommencing.

Twenty minutes later, she couldn't stop staring. It was fascinating. When you knew what you were looking at.

When she approached the dining table a second time, conversation instantly halted. A room of hopeful faces stared back at her. She wished she had better news.

"I figured out the significance of the handkerchiefs. But it doesn't answer all our questions."

"What are they?" asked Marsten.

"A map. Specifically, a map indicating the location of Sam Bass's lost treasure."

Most of the faces around the table looked shocked, but one of the FBI agents just looked confused. "Who's Sam Bass?" he asked.

"Don't mind him," said Ethan. "He's from New Jersey."

Brynnan smiled. "Sam Bass was a notorious outlaw in the eighteen hundreds. Most of his robberies took place in Texas. Texas folklore is full of stories about his supposed buried treasure."

Cole looked skeptical. "No offense, Brynnan, but a map to buried treasure? Isn't that a little..." He was apparently having difficulty choosing a non-offensive word for 'ridiculous.'

But Brynnan wasn't at all offended. "Finding actual treasure? Yes, I agree, I find that unlikely. However, finding a map *claiming* to lead to Sam Bass' treasure is absolutely possible. It's happened before. Several maps claiming to lead to his cache of gold surfaced decades ago, after his death, but I don't believe the others were this detailed. When you place the handkerchiefs on top of each other just right and hold them up to the light, you can see a *labeled* map of Longhorn Caverns on the upper half, indicating a specific spot deep in the cave system. The bottom half details an area two miles west of Round Rock. Both locations correlate with legends about where Sam Bass may have stashed some of his loot. And in the bottom corner, the combined stitches form the year 1878." No one acknowledged the significance of the date, so she added. "That was the year Sam Bass died."

Every expression in the room conveyed varying degrees of confusion. "What I'm saying is," she continued, "this is definitely a map claiming to lead to treasure once belonging to Sam Bass. Whether it's accurate, I have no idea. Whether or not he even actually hid his loot somewhere in Texas, I can't say. I'm just explaining the stitching on the handkerchiefs."

"It definitely sounds significant," said Jack. "But," he looked at Marsten, "does this make any sense to you? Are Hershel or Victor treasure hunters? Would they see something like this and think it's worth killing over?"

The FBI agent from New Jersey didn't give him time to respond. "That doesn't add up to me. Both Hershel and Victor's net worths clock in north of two billion dollars. Why would they need a treasure like that? I don't know what this Bass guy stole, but it wasn't a billion dollars."

"No," said Brynnan. "He was a train robber and held up stagecoaches and banks. But no, even in today's dollars, I wouldn't think it would be an amount that would excite Hershel or Victor."

Marsten shook his head. "They're both opportunists. So, if either of them thought this map was legitimate, yes, they would have it investigated, and they wouldn't think twice about taking any treasure they found. But to hire someone like Nesser? To commit murder? To attack Brynnan?" He turned to the Jersey native. "I agree with you, sir. Even knowing how deplorable and immoral my cousins are, it doesn't make sense to go to these lengths for an alleged treasure of a nineteenth century train robber."

Jack worked his jaw, mulling over the new information. "We may not understand their motivations, but we *know* they both want the handkerchiefs. And, as we were discussing earlier, I don't think they're working together."

The second FBI agent, who'd been glancing at his phone, spoke up for the first time. "This has already been a productive day though. We've been trying to get something concrete on Victor for a while. With everything we learned today, we were able to get a warrant for his house, and I just got a text that the team that went in found the duct tape, zip-tie and broken glass in the room where Brynnan was held. This is huge. Victor will finally have to call his lawyer."

"What about Nesser and the other men he hired?" Brynnan asked, struggling to keep her voice neutral.

"No word on them yet," he replied. "The car they used to chase you around Houston was reported stolen an hour ago. They haven't been spotted. But they will be."

She didn't share his confidence. But she kept her thoughts to herself.

He pocketed his phone and continued. "I think you two," he said, looking at Marsten and Brynnan, "will be safe here tonight. We can post a couple more men out front, just in case, for the night. But tomorrow, go ahead and return home to your ranch. I think Mr. McKerrick can keep you secure there, and we'll stay in contact. Things are starting to unravel. We'll catch these guys soon."

The agents turned their attention to their phones and Marsten left the table looking more frustrated than before. Jack watched him pace in front of the fireplace.

Brynnan gave Jack a helpless shrug. "I don't know why all this is happening. But I'm sure about what that map is *claiming* to be, legitimate or not."

Jack's smile was warm. "You did great. You figured out a huge piece to the puzzle. We just don't know where it fits." Brynnan saw a thought flicker across his face.

"What?"

He stood, and she realized he wanted to move their conversation away from the agents at the table. They walked over to the kitchen and Jack opened the refrigerator. "You want a bottle of water?"

"No, I'm fine. What were you just thinking?"

Jack took a water bottle for himself and turned to face Brynnan. "You figured out what the handkerchiefs mean. I think that's what Victor was afraid of this whole time. I don't think the handkerchiefs would have been an issue except that Marsten sent them to your parents. I think Victor knew the three of you—three historians—would eventually know what you were looking at. And for some reason, that's a huge threat to him."

"But he killed them before they figured out anything." Verbalizing that her parents had been murdered was still surreal. And left her feeling raw. She saw her pain reflected on Jack's face. "I'm okay," she said, with a fortifying breath. "I just mean," she continued, "they didn't know anything, so why kill them?"

Jack hesitated.

She stepped close enough for him to hear her whisper. "Jack, I'm okay. I want to know everything you're thinking. Figuring this out will make me feel better, not ignoring the possibilities. We've been *through* this already."

That drew a half-grin from him. "I know. My point is that when Nesser went to Austin, the only people capable of deciphering the handkerchiefs who had *seen* them, were you and your parents. Maybe Victor thought your parents had already figured it out or were on the verge of deciphering it. Either way, if his fear was someone knowing about the handkerchiefs, then the three of you were dangerous to him."

"I have an idea to that end," Marsten said.

Lost in her thoughts about Jack's words, she hadn't noticed Marsten was now standing next to them. "What? What idea?"

"I was trying to rack my brain as to what could possibly motivate Victor to these lengths. I'm convinced it has to be greed, fear, or more likely, a combination. To be more specific, I think he may be afraid of losing everything."

"Everything? What do you mean?" Jack asked.

"I'll spare you the mindboggling details of the Kade family finances, but suffice it to say that if my Aunt Margaret was to be convinced Victor had stolen any of this Sam Bass treasure and invested it in Kade businesses, he could lose access to his trust fund and be forced to forfeit any profit he ever made from investments of his trust fund. Ever. Basically, he'd be broke."

Brynnan tried wrapping her head around that.

"Um, I don't really understand how trust funds work, I guess. Why would he lose everything? And what does it have to do with your aunt?"

"It's ridiculously complicated, and yet very simple. Trust funds work however the person who establishes them wants them to work. In this case, my grandfather decided on all kinds of rules for the Kade money. One rule being, investing any money in Kade companies that was garnered from theft—say from stagecoach heists—would revoke any Kade their entire trust fund *and* subsequent profits from investments of their trust fund." He leaned forward for emphasis. "Victor would lose billions."

Jack leaned against the kitchen counter. "We don't have proof, but that makes more sense than anything else."

The front door swung open and Marsten's pilot rushed inside. "Sir," he addressed Marsten, but also glanced at Jack. "I was checking over the chopper and found this stuck near the base of one of the skids." He held out a small, black device.

Jack didn't need to study it for more than a second. It was a tracking device. "They know we're here."

"And," the pilot swallowed. "A car just pulled in, as I was running back here."

Everyone started talking at once.

Cole ran in a ducked position beneath the large picture window in the living area, drew up next to it and cautiously peeked around the curtain for a choice view of the sprawling acreage between the cabin and the road. "Yeah, we've got company."

Everyone froze.

He took another look. "Four on foot. And

they're fanning out. Heavily armed. They're surrounding the cabin.

"Marsten and Brynnan," said Jack, "duck down in the kitchen behind the island and stay down."

In a whirl of motion, Marsten drew Brynnan toward the kitchen, while everyone else scattered in synchronized chaos, posting themselves near windows, weapons in hand. Even Marsten's pilot. Brynnan made eye contact as she moved past Jack. "Be careful," she murmured, hoping no one heard the emotion in her voice.

She felt like she and Marsten were in an old western movie, hiding like bartenders behind the bar in a saloon just before the big shoot out.

Adrenaline coursed through her. Her pounding heart felt like it was trying to escape her chest.

Marsten put his arm around her. "I'm sorry Brynnan, you shouldn't have been dragged into this. I love you, sweetheart. And you'll be okay. I promise."

For the first time she noticed Marsten held his own gun.

He shifted her directly behind him.

It hit her then that her uncle was ready and willing to sacrifice himself for her. Anyone who made it into the kitchen would have to shoot him to get to her.

She could hardly breathe.

Tense seconds ticked by.

Ethan spoke up enough for everyone in the cabin to hear. "Let me be clear. There's only one reason these guys would be this bold. They don't plan on letting anyone live. So, if you have a clean shot, take it."

That was the last thing Brynnan heard before she smelled something burning. Desperately praying she was imagining things, she scooted out from behind Marsten just enough to look down the hallway of bedrooms. Reflections of orange light danced on the walls and smoke climbed to the ceiling. "Fire!" she yelled. "The cabin's on fire!"

Jack whipped around and saw the smoke coming from the hallway at the back of the cabin. "Stay low!" he yelled to Marsten and Brynnan. "And come into the living room. We're getting out of here."

"We going for the vehicles?" Cole asked like he was reading Jack's mind.

"I'll head for my dad's SUV. It's the closest. Everyone lay down plenty of cover fire and I'll make a run for it. Send those guys ducking for cover. I'll pull up as close to the door as possible. Brynnan and Marsten jump in first, then everyone else. We cover each other and move fast. That's the plan."

Jack nodded to Cole and Jonas. They were ready to roll. This felt a little like old times. He wasn't sure the FBI agents were keen on taking orders from him, but he took charge first, and really, it was the only viable plan. Besides, he was taking the biggest risk.

He only permitted himself to glance at Brynnan and give her a nod. That took an enormous amount of self-control. But there wasn't time to do what he wanted to do. To rush to her and hold her. To promise her she would be safe even if he had to give his life for her. To kiss her until she wasn't afraid anymore. To tell her he loved her.

Brynnan and Marsten started coughing. Jack's

eyes and throat started to burn. Time to go.

CHAPTER THIRTEEN

Brynnan watched Jack open the front door, and everything afterward unfolded in slow motion, like a dream—or a nightmare. Deafening gunfire erupted all around her. Jack rushed out, firing as he ran, all the way to the SUV.

He spent no more than ten seconds running to the SUV, starting the engine and driving it within inches of the cabin's front porch, but they were the most excruciating ten seconds of her life.

The barrage of bullets assaulting the SUV and the cabin unnerved her. She wasn't sure if she screamed or not. She wouldn't have heard it over the storm of gunfire. And the blaze devouring the bedrooms was threatening to enter the living area. She saw flames licking the ceiling near the sofa where Jack had kissed her. Really kissed her, with more emotion behind his kiss than there'd been before. Smoke stung her eyes and her chest heaved for air.

She was terrified. Again. But this time, she wasn't scared for herself. She wasn't thinking about what might happen to her. She was afraid for Jack—him getting hurt, or killed. That was her worst nightmare now.

She prayed a different scripture this time. *The Lord is my strength and my shield; my heart trusts in him, and he helps me.* She knew God wasn't a genie in a bottle that you just wished to for safety or luck, but she knew her prayers were always heard, and that God always answered, even if His answer looked different than what she thought she wanted. She prayed again and again in those precious seconds for the Lord to be Jack's strength and shield. She desperately hoped Jack would survive unscathed. But what she wanted more than anything was God's protection over his heart and soul.

A peace blossomed within her.

She still had no idea if they'd survive this battle physically, but she knew God was with them.

Marsten wrapped his arm around her waist as they ran out the door, shielding her from the gunmen's aim. Jumping in the SUV, she made eye contact with Jack just long enough for him to motion for them to stay down. They crouched on the floor behind the second row of captain's chairs to make room for the others to pile in. Cole brought up the rear, being the ninth full grown adult to cram into the seven-passenger vehicle. Jack hit the gas.

"Everybody ok?" Jack asked.

"All in one piece," Cole answered. "Those guys are crazy, but not the best marksmen."

Ethan kept an eye on the gunmen through the back windshield. "They're following."

"I figured that," Jack said. He made eye contact with the agent from New Jersey in the rearview mirror. "Think you guys can set up a roadblock for me to lead them into?"

Jersey grinned. And Jack realized he was already on his cell. "Way ahead of you."

Minutes later, on a rural road between a hilly meadow and wooded area, Jack lured their pursuers to the authorities ready with spike strips. Jack drove past, and the spike strips were deployed. Nesser and his men never had a chance.

Brynnan watched swarms of law enforcement descend on the car of mercenaries with four flat tires. No one would escape today.

The men around her started to unpack themselves from the overcrowded, bullet riddled SUV. When she finally exited, she hugged her uncle, whom she now knew she could trust with her life. Then looked around for Jack.

Someone wearing an FBI vest had stopped him to ask a question. He answered, looked around, and he headed straight for her. His eyes scoured her as he walked up, but not in a lustful way. Worry poured off of him as he searched for any signs of injury.

"Hey, I'm alright," she said.

"Your eyes are red."

"Well, there was a lot of smoke, but I'll live." Unfortunately, her body chose that moment to start coughing. She cleared her throat, afraid she wasn't selling the 'I'm fine' image very well. "Really, I'm okay. Are you?"

"Yes. I'll see if I can find you some water. Maybe one of the squad cars—"

"Wait." She looked at the four gunmen. The four kidnappers. At least one murderer. They were cuffed, but not in squad cars yet. "Can we talk to them?"

Jack's eyebrows shot up.

"*What? Are you serious?* You're not going anywhere near them."

He came off a little commanding, but she let it go, since he'd been in soldier mode just minutes before.

"Yes, I'm serious. We need to know—*I have to know*—for sure why my parents were killed. *He's right there*. He might not answer me, but maybe he'll say something."

Maybe it was the adrenaline, or the drama of the past two weeks, or needing closure that bolstered her, but for some reason, she felt no fear in walking straight up to Nesser, which she started to do.

She made two full strides in his direction before Jack cut her off and gripped her upper arms.

"No way. This is *not* a good idea," he said.

The motion apparently caught Nesser's attention because he suddenly looked in Brynnan's direction. Glaring, from twenty yards away. She glared back.

Jack was about to lose his mind. He'd done everything he possibly could to keep this woman safe from Nesser, including running through gunfire to help them all escape a burning cabin, and now she wanted to walk right up to him. Yes, he was cuffed. And they were surrounded by dozens of law enforcement officers. But still.

Apparently, they'd gained Jack's dad's attention too. "What's going on?" Ethan asked, walking over.

Jack loosened his grip on Brynnan but moved to block her line of sight to Nesser. "She wants to interrogate your prisoner."

Brynnan's face still looked more determined than Jack was comfortable with. Ethan raised an eyebrow. "Really? Well, I understand your need for answers. But I promise you he'll be questioned. He'll probably lawyer up, but we have so much on him, he won't be a free man any time soon."

She wasn't appeased. "But there's still so much we don't know. Like why the handkerchiefs are such a threat to Victor, why he murdered my parents, and why he came after me." She shifted her stance to make eye contact with Nesser again. His furious glare reconnected with hers and, though Jack tried to reassure himself that looks couldn't actually kill, he pivoted to block the vehement staring battle.

Jack watched her pull her attention back to him. He saw so much frustration and emotion storming behind those beautiful eyes. He wished he could solve everything, make her feel safe and content. But he could never bring her parents back. Or erase the terror she'd experienced.

All he could manage was what came out sounding like a throaty, desperate plea. "Bryn...please..."

Her expression softened a small fraction. She balled her fists and tensed. It was another one of those moments where he wasn't sure if she was going to hit him or cry. Again, he'd rather she hit him.

She stormed off in the opposite direction.

His dad clamped a hand down on his shoulder. "I like her," he said, with a huge grin on his face.

Jack let out a long breath. "I'm glad. She's making me crazy, but—"

Shots rang out. One. Two. A third shot.

Frenzied chaos ensued as everyone drew weapons, ran for cover, shouted orders and tried to pinpoint the source of the shooting.

Jack saw one of Nesser's accomplices on the ground, his vacant eyes staring skyward. A second accomplice laid in a pool of blood. Someone was sniping the mercenaries before they could talk. Before they could testify against Victor.

Brynnan. Where was she? Victor was apparently desperate enough to send someone to assassinate his loose ends *while they were in federal custody,* and Jack was sure he didn't want Brynnan to live long enough to decipher the handkerchiefs. Of course, she'd already done it, and announced her findings, but Victor didn't know that.

He darted around the emergency vehicles in a crouched position, weapon drawn, searching for Brynnan, and the shooter. He found the shooter first.

A sniper rifle hung on his back and gripping a handgun, he raced like lightning through the tall grass to a car, partially hidden in the trees. He noticed Jack and slowed. Lifted his sidearm and aimed. Jack fired first.

A small army of police and FBI descended on their position, shouting orders in every direction. The sniper was dead.

A sick dread roiled in Jack. There had been three shots. *Three.*

Hopefully one was a miss.

He had to find Brynnan. He ran back into the crowd on the street, spun in a circle and, deciding she hadn't rejoined the scene in the road, he ran in the direction she'd headed in her frustration minutes earlier.

He tried to ignore the perfect line of sight the sniper would have had on Brynnan.

He jumped a ditch and tore through the wooded area yelling her name. The waning sunlight made it difficult to see. *"Bryn! Bryn!"* Still no answer. Maybe he missed her on the road. But he was sure he hadn't. Dread pricked every nerve in his body. Something was very wrong.

He prayed the most earnest prayer he'd ever prayed.

God please, please help me find her. Alive. Please God, please lead me to her, and let her be okay.

He noticed a crumpled form on the ground just a few yards away. Light pink blouse.

He rushed to her side so quickly he almost couldn't stop his momentum from carrying him straight into her. He crashed to his knees beside her still body. Too still.

No, no, no. Please no.

He felt for a pulse and felt a steady beat. *Thank you, God, thank you.*

He choked on the emotion in his throat, wanting to surrender to relief. But she was unconscious.

Blood oozed from her arm. Definitely from a bullet, but it looked superficial.

Dozens of rocks laid around her in what looked like a dried-up creek. She must have fallen when the bullet caught her arm and hit her head on a rock. He didn't see any abrasions on her forehead, so he gingerly slid his fingers around the side and back of her head, wishing he was running his fingers through her hair in a much, much different scenario.

He found a large lump on the side of her head. She moaned.

"Bryn? Can you hear me?"

She moaned again and her eyes fluttered open.

"What...Jack? What happened?" She started to move and winced.

"Hey, hey, stay still. Tell me how you feel. Can you move your legs? Is anything broken?"

"Hmm? No, just...ow, my arm. And...oh, my head. What happened?"

Relief flooded through him now, stealing his voice. He noticed he was trembling and didn't care. He leaned over her and kissed her forehead, then brushed his lips across hers. "Baby, you scared me to death."

He pulled back enough to watch her eyes fill with warmth as she took in his words, and his tender tone.

He pulled some dried leaves from her hair. "How about we get you out of here?"

"Sounds good." She tried to get up and winced again.

"I've got you," he said, gripping her healthy arm.

"Truer words were never spoken."

Shock spread across his face at her quick response. "Really?" He shook his head. "I'd like to believe that, but it'll sound better when I'm sure you don't have a concussion."

He pulled her to her feet, and she stood on her own for a whole two seconds before she fell into him, gripping her head.

"Um...about that concussion...are we surrounded by fireflies, or am I seeing stars?"

"Okay, you're not walking out of here. Just hang on, the ambulance is still back at the scene. I'll have you there in less than a minute." He didn't give her a chance to discuss it. He picked her up, gently cradling her across his chest, and headed for the road.

She started to protest but, decided against it. Her head really, really hurt. And her arm was throbbing. And she really didn't mind being in Jack's arms.

She knew everything wasn't completely resolved with Victor or the relevant dangers, but things could be worse. She allowed her head to loll against Jack's neck. *This amazing man. Yep, things could be worse.* She was more convinced now that Jack was a gift from God. A precious gift she was determined not to take for granted.

CHAPTER FOURTEEN

An hour later, Brynnan was sitting in a hospital in College Station. She didn't like the idea of being in a hospital again, a week and a half after her parents' deaths—*had it really only been that long?*—but she didn't disagree that she needed to go. The bullet only grazed her arm, but it was still bleeding. And it hurt. She didn't mind something to numb the pain.

But when the doctor insisted she be admitted overnight for observation for a concussion, she was frustrated. And her pathetic plea to the doctor was embarrassing. She attempted to argue with him but talking made her head hurt worse and she winced from the pain, invalidating all her appeal.

Marsten, Cole and Jack accompanied her to the hospital, but after she got settled in a room, she assured Marsten she was fine and told him to go home.

"Are you sure you're feeling better? Do you need anything?" he asked.

"No, honestly Marsten, I'm fine. Go home and get some sleep."

He smiled and patted her leg. "Alright,

sweetheart, but I asked Jack to stay with you tonight. I don't suppose you mind that?" He winked at her.

Apparently, Marsten's not in the dark about anything.

And he seemed happy about it.

She realized just then how much his approval meant to her personally, but it also occurred to her that, as Jack's boss *and* her uncle, it was probably a really good thing that he was pleased.

"No, I don't mind at all. Thank you," she answered with a smile. "By the way, where *is* Jack?"

"Right here," he said, entering the room carrying two large drinks. "I found a smoothie place downstairs. Do you want blueberry banana or strawberry orange?"

This man is almost too perfect. She nearly told him right then and there that she loved him. But that would've been awkward. "Oh, thank you. Those look fantastic. Both sound good. I'll take the blueberry banana though."

"Alright," Marsten said, "I think you're well taken care of for now. Call me as soon as you talk to the doctor in the morning. Hopefully, you'll be home by lunch. I know Annalee will make you anything in the world you want to eat. She's so concerned about you. She told me to tell you she's praying for you."

"That's so sweet of her. Please tell her thank you. I'm sure I'll be back tomorrow."

"I'm sure you will. I'll see you then." He patted her leg one last time and turned to leave. On his way out, he faced Jack. "You take care of our girl."

"Yes, sir."

Marsten smiled and left the room.

Brynnan and Jack were alone for the first time since before the helicopter landed at the cabin.

For about five seconds.

A knock sounded at the door, and a cheerful nurse breezed in introducing herself and checking on Brynnan's needs.

Jack took a step back to allow the nurse to take Brynnan's vitals. He watched her lay in the hospital bed looking so vulnerable, but brave. Tired, but beautiful. Weary, yet resilient.

A rapid-fire deluge of thoughts flooded him while the nurse performed her duties.

He knew how he felt. He had no doubts. But should he tell her everything now? Was it too soon? Did she feel as deeply as he did? She'd been through so much. Maybe she just saw him as a rescuer from all the trauma of the past several days. He sensed more, but he didn't want to rush her. He wanted to do this right. He didn't want her to have any doubts. Or regrets.

When the nurse finally left, Jack stood next to Brynnan's bed. He casually asked how she liked her smoothie and how she was feeling, but there was so much more behind his eyes.

"What's wrong?" she asked.

He stroked her arm with his fingertips. "I nearly lost you today. More than once. I should have anticipated more. I should have checked—"

"Stop. Just stop. None of this was your fault. You were up against a small army of lunatics. No one could have anticipated their plan. The truth is, I haven't thanked you enough. I took you for granted, especially in the beginning. That first night, when the shooter...when he... I was so absorbed with the loss of my parents. I don't know if I even thanked you for saving my life. I remember you shielding me on the floor, and I remember you holding me afterwards. I was so overwhelmed, I didn't even recognize how much I appreciated you that night."

She caught his fingers resting on her arm and squeezed them. "But I do now. You're amazing. Thank you."

She was undoing him. He was tempted to propose to her in his next breath. But her look of admiration had morphed into longing. His eyes went to her lips. And a force he knew he'd never tire of drew him to her.

And another knock at the door. *Seriously? Are they kidding?* He'd give his first big paycheck for thirty minutes alone with this woman right now. *I wonder if that door has a 'do not disturb' sign. Or a lock.*

No one entered. He guessed it wasn't a nurse and walked to the door. When he opened the door, his father stood in the hallway.

"I know Brynnan needs her rest, but I have some things I thought she might want to hear."

That sounded promising.

Seeing Ethan walk in, Brynnan's eyebrows shot up before worry drew them together. "Hello." She pulled the thin blanket up to her chest and tried to sit up a little straighter. "I can't thank you enough for your help today. But you look like you have news."

"Yes, I do. But first, how are you?"

His concern warmed her. Ethan's compassion

had a familiar ring to it. "I'm fine. I wish I didn't need to stay here tonight, but I'm sure they'll let me go tomorrow."

"Well, I'm glad they're being cautious. A concussion can be serious. How's the arm?"

"Still numb. I'm sure I'll feel it later." She tried to keep her impatience out of her voice but, why had he come?

Jack shifted his weight. She could tell he was eager for answers too. "So, what don't we know?"

"Well, first of all, Victor is in custody. We're questioning Hershel too, but he and his lawyer are insisting he didn't have knowledge of how Victor was handling things, so I'm not sure how that's going to turn out. Victor called his lawyer too, but we have *plenty* on him after today. He won't be bothering you anytime soon. He's not talking yet, of course, but it doesn't matter."

"Why?" Jack and Brynnan asked in unison.

"Well, apparently, the sniper attack was the tipping point."

Brynnan was confused. "I thought Jack—"

"Yes," Ethan nodded, "Jack got him. The sniper is dead. But his actions prompted Nesser's sole surviving accomplice to start talking. When he realized Victor sent a sniper to tie up loose ends, including *him*, he decided cooperating with us was his best bet. We promised him a few concessions, and safety, in exchange for everything he knew. And it was a lot."

Brynnan's eyes grew wide. "What did he tell you?"

"Marsten was on the right track about Victor's and Hershel's motivations. Apparently, they came across the map you deciphered decades ago. And they followed the top portion to a significant amount of money buried deep in Longhorn Caverns."

"Seriously? It was really there? Sam Bass's treasure...I can't believe it. That's incredible. All this time..." *Wow.* For a couple of seconds, she forgot about the tragic events surrounding them. Finding some, if not all, of Sam Bass's loot right where a map from 1878 said it would be was a significant historical discovery.

But the moment passed. The reason she was sitting in a hospital bed smothered her excitement for the slice of Texas history transforming from legend to fact. "Sorry, go ahead."

"Oh, it's fascinating, I know. I have a buddy who's a treasure hunter. He's going to flip when this finally comes out. But as far as the Kades go, it gets more interesting. Apparently, Hershel's brother, Eugene, found out about the Bass money, and that Victor and Hershel had invested it in Kade businesses. He doesn't report it to authorities, of course, he instead runs to Aunt Margaret and tells her, hoping Hershel and Victor will lose all their inheritance and he'll get it instead."

"Nice family," Brynnan said.

"Yeah," Ethan nodded. "So, the way our informant understands it, Aunt Margaret took Victor and Hershel's side and refused to believe the money was stolen unless Eugene could prove Victor and Hershel had the map. Eugene didn't know where they kept the map. Victor thought they got away with it. Hershel had the map, so Victor told him to burn it."

"But Hershel didn't burn it," Jack said.

"Nope. He decided it was a lucky charm.

Seriously, the guy said Hershel kept it 'for good luck.'" He shook his head. "Our present trouble started when Hershel had some remodeling done. A housekeeper of his, tasked with removing some of his belongings for safe keeping, stored the handkerchiefs in a box in his boat in the garage."

"And Hershel sold the boat to Victor," Jack finished the story for him.

"Yes. Ironic. Since it was Victor who accidently sent the handkerchiefs to Marsten. He didn't check the boxes very carefully. Once Hershel realized what happened and told Victor and Victor realized Marsten had the boxes..."

"Victor called Nesser," Jack said.

"But why not just ask for the boxes back? Why immediately employ someone like Nesser?"

Ethan sighed. "Good question. My guess is they didn't want any attention called to the handkerchiefs, if they could avoid it. I believe they thought revealing that they wanted them back would make Marsten take a closer look at them. And then they would be in very real danger of losing everything. And when Victor realized you and your parents saw the contents of the boxes, our informant says Victor went nuts because he was sure your parents or you could decipher the map."

"He was right about that part," Jack said, half his mouth tweaking up.

"True," Ethan said, with a respectful dip of his head to Brynnan.

She didn't deserve it though. Didn't deserve the impressed look on Jack's face either. If she or her parents had figured out the relevance of the handkerchiefs when the boxes first arrived, maybe they would still be alive. It had taken her too long.

She'd zoned out for a second, but apparently Ethan was still talking.

"Nesser has acted as Victor's 'fixer' before. And Nesser has no regard for human life, he just wants the job done—an attitude he seems to share with Victor."

"That answers most of it," Jack said, "but I thought this had something to do with the Alesi family. At Victor's, we heard them talking about one of the guys wanting to exact revenge on Bobby Alesi."

Ethan nodded. "Nesser was Victor's contact in hiring the rest of the mercenaries. We're learning more about Nesser. Let's just say he's traveled in the same circles as the Alesi family enough to know who has a grudge against Bobby."

"So those are the men he zeroed in on to help him with Victor's mess," Jack said.

"Yes," Ethan nodded, his eyes a familiar mix of seriousness and concern locking with Brynnan's. "We're told they were hired because they were especially motivated to get to Rachel, and to you. I don't say that to scare you, but given the circumstances, I believe it's best you stay aware of all possible threats."

Threats that are *still* out there. Always will be. That knocked the air out of her lungs.

She nodded that she understood, but fears, new and old, ran like ice through her veins, freezing her voice.

Jack was staring at her. She wasn't hiding her unease very well.

Ethan must have sensed he needed to leave.

"Well, I hope having some answers will help you rest tonight."

"Yes. Yes, thank you, Ethan. I appreciate you coming by. Thank you," Brynnan said, hoping her fears didn't muffle the sincerity of her gratitude. She liked Jack's dad. And she was grateful for the information, but she had a lot to think about. To pray about.

Jack thanked his dad as well, and walked him to the door. Brynnan heard them exchange goodbyes and then Jack was back by her side, looking right through her.

He laced his fingers through hers and sat on the side of the bed. "What's wrong?"

She tried to reign in her emotions. "Jack," her voice cracked.

So much for reigning in the emotion.

"Victor may not be a threat anymore, but I'll be in danger because of the Alesis forever. It will never end. I denied that for a while. But I can't any longer. I shouldn't. It doesn't matter that I don't associate with them. What they've done, and are still doing, may put me in danger...and anyone I care about. I... I couldn't handle it if something happened to you because of me."

That didn't seem to faze him. Was he listening?

"Brynnan, you're not telling me anything I don't know."

He rubbed his thumb in circles on the back of her hand. Oh, this man. Didn't he see how damaged she was? And how the past would never really stay in the past? Not as long as she was Bobby Alesi's granddaughter. Not to mention the apparent danger in being Marsten Kade's niece.

"I just hope you're thinking straight. I'm related to the Kade family *and* the Alesi family. Marsten aside, that doesn't paint a very pretty picture."

He slid his hand away from hers and she was surprised how much she instantly missed even that small touch. He fixed his eyes on her, but she couldn't read them. She braced herself for what he was about to say.

"You're right. Partly. Look, I know you value the truth and feel more comfortable knowing all the facts, even if they're difficult."

"Yes." She did. Absolutely. But...if he was about to end things...break off what was growing between them...she suddenly wasn't sure she could bear it. But that was selfish. If she cared about this man, and she knew she did, she should want something better for him. Some*one* better for him, better than her, with all her issues.

He squared his shoulders to fully face her. *Don't look at his broad shoulders...or his muscular chest...or his toned arms...*She focused on his eyes. *Ugh. Those eyes make me weaker than anything else...Dear Lord, if he's about to sever whatever is between us, please give me strength...I'm afraid it will crush me.*

"You okay?" he asked.

Depends on what you're about to say. "Yes, I'm fine. You were saying?"

"I'm saying, the truth is, I agree the Alesis may continually put you in danger. And I have more than a small amount of concern about the Kades. They're greedy, unethical, and incredibly wealthy. That's a dangerous combination. I trust Marsten, but with reservation."

"What do you mean by that?" She didn't blame him. She wasn't sure she could trust Marsten until today. When he risked his life for hers. But why was Jack hesitant?

He placed his palms on his thighs with a deep sigh. "I can tell your uncle has a complicated past. One he's reticent about. I don't have any proof, but I sense he has a lot of secrets. And possibly enemies. I'm not saying he's one of the bad guys. I'm just saying..."

"There are probably more things he's kept from me. And you. Like how he knows Bobby Alesi so well," she whispered, finishing his thought.

"Yeah."

She met his eyes. And she saw his mind switch gears. He wasn't thinking about Marsten anymore.

"The other truth you need to hear is...that I care about you. Hopefully, you've figured that out."

He fought the urge to touch her. He needed to get this out. Needed to find the right words. "We've been through a lot in the past week or so. I hate that you went through any of it, truly, but the silver lining is that it showed me what kind of woman you are when things get tough, how strong your faith is." He visibly swallowed. "I know how I feel. But I want to give you time to process everything."

"Process everything?" What did he mean? If he expected a few days to erase all the pain...that wasn't going to happen. "Jack, if you're talking about completely processing my parents' deaths, being shot at in their home, Nesser breaking into my bedroom, being...being...kidnapped again, getting shot... Jack, I may wrestle with all of that for the rest of my life. I told you, I still have nightmares about when I was kidnapped years ago. I've learned to trust God with those things. So, it should be easier this time but, still..."

"I know. I deal with my own issues, remember?" His voice was barely above a whisper and riding a tidal wave of emotion. "Please don't try to carry that burden on your own—grappling with death and fear and evil can consume you unless you surrender it all to Jesus. Try to release it to Him."

He gently held her hands in his, but the intensity of his hoarse whisper pulsated through his touch. "We're not promised an easy life, it rarely is. But God's still sovereign. And you can trust Him to sustain you, no matter what happens. *Do not be anxious about anything, but in every situation, by prayer and petition, with thanksgiving, present your requests to God. And the peace of God, which transcends all understanding, will guard your hearts and your minds in Christ Jesus.*"

Tears poured down her cheeks. She knew the truth when she heard it. She'd read it so many times studying God's word, but *completely* trusting God with all her fears and guilt from the past had been terrifying—to give away that much control, *all* control... She hadn't meant for the barriers she put up—to protect her from people—to also keep her Lord from her whole heart, but now she realized they had.

Hearing Jack speak the words out loud bolstered her courage to embrace—to *fully* embrace—the peace God had been offering all along. Emotion crashed through her.

Jack pulled her to him, wrapping her in his

arms, smoothing her hair, feeling the tension release from her body as she quietly sobbed on his shoulder. He tried to swallow his own emotion. He knew her battle. Far too well. The evil in this world had stolen his peace in the past.

She buried her head in the crook of his neck, relaxing against him as her tears subsided, her breath tickling his skin. "I know, I do trust Him. God's strength is infinite," she whispered.

She sat up to look into his eyes. "I know I'm truly strong only when I'm leaning completely on Him. I've known that ever since I came to Christ. I have a lot more to trust Him with now, but I know I'm safe in His hands."

She looked at him with the strangest expression, and suddenly he was afraid she was reading his mind.

She smiled and touched his face. "You're safe in His hands too, you know. You don't need to carry the weight of this job, or of your past, on your own either."

He placed his hand over hers, pressing it against his face. "You mean, take my own advice?"

"Yeah, something like that."

He gently brushed the straggling tears from her face. He wasn't going to start expecting life to be easy, but he could already tell Brynnan was helping him be the man God wanted him to be.

He prayed God would allow him to marry her.

She cocked her head, narrowing her eyes at him. "Why the smile? What are you thinking about?"

His smile broadened. "One step at a time."

"What's that supposed to mean?"

"A minute ago, I was trying to say, that I want to give you time to process whether or not you want to be with *me*. As more than your security detail," he added with a grin. "I don't want to rush you. I just want to give you time...to think about it, pray about it."

Oh.

Everything inside her melted. She didn't deserve this man. And yet, everything about him felt right.

So. Right.

"Yes, I absolutely want to be with you."

And I trust you. That was the real truth. The crucial truth. Suddenly, recognition dawned. She'd been telling God she trusted Him all this time but had been scared to do everything He asked. And now she knew, trusting God with her heart meant trusting Jack with her heart.

Her insides were bursting. "And I don't need any time to process that."

"Really?"

She saw his eyes fill with surprise. Then relief. Then tenderness.

His gaze held hers for about two beats, then the distance between them disappeared. His kiss was strong. Hungry. Emotional.

She lost all sense of time. After an eternity, but way too soon, Jack placed his palms on her pillow on either side of her head and pushed himself back, a little out of breath, just far enough to look her in the eyes.

Which took an extraordinary amount of self-control. But he was determined to be the gentleman worthy of this amazing woman. Brynnan was perfect for him. He knew it in his heart and soul. He had no doubts, but he knew it had happened fast. He should probably ask her out before he bought a ring. Which he planned to do soon.

He broke into his most charming smile. "Does this mean if I ask you out on a date, you'll say yes?"

"A date?"

"Yeah, you know, like normal people do. When they're not being shot at. Could I take you out to dinner some night this week Miss Marsh?"

She may have giggled. Which was kind of embarrassing. And kind of cute. "Yes. Absolutely yes."

Another knock at the door. Another nurse.

When she was finished with her tasks and bid them a cheery goodbye, Jack returned to his spot, sitting on the edge of her bed. "You know, I'll need to talk to Marsten. About us. He mentioned a week or so ago that he wouldn't mind it if I was 'interested in you' but—"

"What? Are you serious? He said that a week ago?"

Jack nodded. "Oh yeah. It was awkward."

"I'm sure it was. But he didn't act like he disapproved a few minutes ago. I know he didn't say anything, but he implied he knew…"

"I know. But I don't want to assume too much. I want to do this right. I'm going to tell him I'll resign if he's not comfortable with his head of security courting his niece."

Whoa. She didn't see that coming. It made sense but… "Are you sure? You're *good* at this job.

Marsten needs you. And...and I don't want you to resent—"

"I won't resent you. That's not going to happen. I'm saying you're more important to me than having this job. Not that I want to quit. I don't. I want it to work. But I want you to know that will have to be Marsten's decision."

Wow. His integrity moved her. "You're a good man, Jack McKerrick."

He heard the sincerity in her words. She hadn't uttered them flippantly. He felt a deep longing to live up to that compliment, every single day.

Dear God, please help me be the man she deserves, the man You want me to be for her.

Never before had she allowed her heart to be so exposed, so vulnerable. But she trusted the Lord's prodding. An overwhelming peace that God had guided her straight to Jack, had guided them both to each other, wrapped around her like a warm blanket. The world was still a dangerous, scary place but, the tenderness and commitment in Jack's eyes obliterated her fears about trusting him with her heart.

She reached up with her arm—the one that wasn't throbbing from a bullet wound—fisted his shirt and pulled him to her.

He smiled and eagerly complied. Slipping his fingers into her hair—careful not to touch her bruise—he cradled her head and possessed her lips. The fervor and burning intensity of his kiss was unlike anything she'd felt before—sending a beautiful heat searing through her entire body.

She felt the current passing between them carrying so much more than passion—everything in his touch reverberated with hope and promise. A promise she could count on. Forever.

Made in the USA
Columbia, SC
19 July 2024

38955761R00153